APR 1 4 1996

W9-BLF-385

Dancing *on the*
Bridge *of* Avignon

Dancing *on the* Bridge *of* Avignon

Ida Vos

Translated by Terese Edelstein and Inez Smidt

RETA E. KING LIBRARY
CHADRON STATE COLLEGE
CHADRON. NE 69337

Houghton Mifflin Company
Boston 1995

Copyright © 1989 by Ida Vos
First American edition 1995
Originally published in the Netherlands in 1989 by Uitgeverij Leopold
Translation by Terese Edelstein and Inez Smidt copyright © 1995 by
Houghton Mifflin Company

All rights reserved. For information about permission to
reproduce selections from this book, write to Permissions,
Houghton Mifflin Company, 215 Park Avenue South,
New York, New York 10003.

Library of Congress Cataloging-in-Publication Data

Vos, Ida, 1931–
    [Dansen op de brug van Avignon. English]
    Dancing on the bridge of Avignon/by Ida Vos; translated by
Terese Edelstein and Inez Smidt.
        p.   cm.
    Summary: Relates the experiences of a young Jewish girl and her
family during the Nazi occupation of the Netherlands.
    ISBN 0-395-72039-7
    1. World War, 1939–1945—Netherlands—Juvenile fiction.   2. Jews—
Netherlands—Juvenile fiction.   [1. World War, 1939–1945—
Netherlands—Fiction.   2. Jews—Netherlands—Fiction.
    3. Netherlands—History—German occupation, 1940–1945—Fiction.]
    I. Edelstein, Terese.   II. Smidt, Inez.   III. Title.
PZ7.V9718Dan   1995   94-44638
[Fic]—dc20   CIP
                           AC

Printed in the United States of America
BP   10   9   8   7   6   5   4   3   2   1

Also by Ida Vos

Hide and Seek
Anna Is Still Here

For Micha Moskovic and Amit Vos

◆ Boots

Rosa de Jong dreams during the daytime. Before the war, she dreamed only at night. But now she often sits down in her father's big chair, puts her thumb in her mouth, and begins to dream.

She knows that it is babyish to suck your thumb, but she doesn't care. Dreams come more easily with a thumb in your mouth, even if you *are* ten years old.

"Go out in the sun," her mother keeps telling her. "Why can't you be more like your sister? Silvie is only seven, but she likes to be outside."

"I don't," Rosa wants to say, but she doesn't dare. She wishes that Mama would stop nagging her.

What would she do outside? The non-Jewish children who were her classmates at the Beetslaan School no longer talk to her. Surely they think that speaking to a Jewish child is forbidden by the Germans. Yesterday, when Rosa was sitting on the fence in front of the music school, she saw Martha walking by. "Hello, Martha!" she shouted, but Martha didn't answer. She merely looked at her.

"Go to hell!" Rosa called softly, but Martha was already past. She spit in Martha's direction. A big white glob landed on the sidewalk. Berend, a boy from the neighborhood, saw it.

"Keep your Jewish glue to yourself, you filthy cow!" he shouted, and Rosa moved out of his way just in time. If she hadn't run inside so quickly, he would have punched her in the nose. She knows that for sure.

"I'm never going outside again," she told her mother. "Never again."

"Oh, come on," Mama answered quietly. "Who knows how much longer you'll be able to go out? Who knows what else the Germans will do to add to our misery? Go out and enjoy the sun while you still can."

"I just want to dream," Rosa whispered. She put her thumb in her mouth, and curled up in the big chair.

Rosa de Jong dreams during the daytime.

She is walking down a long street. It's hot. The street is empty. There isn't a tree in sight. Rosa would like to skip, but she can't; it feels as though her white sandals are glued to the sidewalk. What can be the matter with them? Are there pebbles inside? She sits down on a bench, and takes off her sandals. When she puts her hand inside one, she feels that the bottom is covered with very sharp pins. It's no wonder she can hardly walk. She'll have to continue in her bare feet, for she never wants to wear those sandals again!

The street feels warm under her feet. She can walk quite easily now; she is practically floating. She approaches a deserted bus stop. Although no one is standing nearby, something does seem to be waiting for the bus, something strange. At first Rosa thinks it might be a dog, but when she looks carefully, she sees that it is a pair of black boots. Surely someone has just stepped out of them. Cautiously she moves toward them. She looks inside the left boot, and sees that it is lined with bright-green velvet.

She doesn't understand how it happens, but suddenly the boots are on her feet, and she takes a few steps. She can walk very well in them, even though they are much too big for her.

Left, right, left, right. Rosa is marching just like a soldier. The boots make a clicking sound against the cobblestones.

Suddenly she realizes that she has left her white sandals behind. She turns pale with fright. Perhaps she left them at the bus stop. She will have to go back and get them, for if she returns home without her sandals, she will certainly be punished.

The boots keep marching, with Rosa's feet still inside. She sees her white sandals in the distance. Another couple of steps and she will be able to get them.

Someone has appeared at the bus stop! A man. A man in a uniform, with a helmet on his head. A German. Rosa doesn't want to continue but she must, for the boots are walking on their own.

When she approaches the German, she can see that he is thrashing all about. He jumps into the air, then comes back down. "Ow!" he screams when he lands.

Rosa looks at his feet. The soldier is wearing her sandals! No wonder he is crying out. The pins are pricking the soles of his feet.

"*Hilfe!*" he shouts. "*Hilfe!*" Rosa knows that *hilfe* is the German word for "help."

Is the soldier looking at her? Is he going to shoot? Rosa would like to hide, but she would not fit behind the sign at the bus stop. If only there were some trees along this peculiar street!

"*Hilfe!*" he shouts again, and jumps into the air. Rosa puts up her hand to shield her eyes from the sun. Where is the German? It's taking him a long time to come back down.

"*Hilfe!*" he calls from the clouds. "*Hilfe!*"

"No!" Rosa shouts. "I'm not going to help you. You can explode into pieces up there in the sky. Go take my sandals and burst into pieces, and never come back to this street again!"

She can't help laughing at the Nazi who is bursting apart. She laughs so hard that tears are streaming down her cheeks.

"Rosa, stop that idiotic laughing!" Someone is tugging on her sleeve. "Stop it, Rosa!"

She opens one eye and sees that it is her father who is nearly pulling the sleeve off her blouse.

"Stop it!" he repeats.

"Have *you* ever seen a Nazi burst into pieces?" she asks, still laughing.

"Stop it, Rosa. You've been making me crazy lately. Ever since the Germans fired me from my job I've been out of sorts, anyway, and now this...I don't know where to begin with you and your dreaming." He slaps her hard across her face. "Stop it! You're driving me crazy!"

"Leave me alone!" she shouts. "You shouldn't hit me!"

"Rosa, what's the matter?" Mother is now in the room, too.

"Papa hit me because a Nazi exploded into pieces. Have *you* ever seen a Nazi blow up? Well, *I* have. He split open in the sky, just like that."

"You've been dreaming, Rosa." Mother strokes her head.

"I know. I do it on purpose."

"I have an idea," says her mother. "I'll go get your violin. I heard you play so beautifully yesterday. Play that piece by Rieding again for me. You can dream while you are playing the violin, too."

"No, I want to sit here and sleep."

"Leave her alone," she hears her mother say to her father. "Actually, I don't blame her. It's so difficult to be awake these days."

Rosa puts her thumb back in her mouth and continues to dream.

◆ *Silvie Dreams, Too*

"Rosa, Mama told me to tell you that you have to either go outside or play your violin," Silvie says, and she crawls into the chair with her sister.

"Won't you go outside?" Silvie asks.

"No, I'm dreaming."

"May I dream with you?"

"All right."

"Shall we dream that we had a radio again? That the Nazis didn't make us turn our radio in?"

"All right."

"We used to listen to Jacob Hamel's Children's Choir on Tuesday afternoons," Silvie says, and begins to sing:

> *Twice a week I take a bath,*
> *Boys, boys, what a lot of fun is that.*

She grabs Rosa by the chin. "Sing with me!"

"Leave me alone."

"I've thought of a wonderful dream." Silvie moves closer to her sister. "I'm going to the library, and there is no sign saying FORBIDDEN FOR JEWS in front of it. The librarian walks up to me and says that I may take out all the books I want. I sit on the floor and read, and no one comes by to say that I shouldn't be there because I'm Jewish. After I've chosen enough books, I walk home, just like that, right through the park, and there's no sign there, either. I don't look back, not even once, because I'm not afraid that someone will say, 'What are *you* doing here? Jewish children aren't allowed in the park.' And that's what I'm going to dream."

Silvie closes her eyes and puts her thumb halfway in her mouth. She drools a bit. Her head rests on Rosa's shoulder. "That dream about the library and the park won't come," she says. "And I want it to so much."

"Just sit still. That's what I always do. Don't move," says Rosa.

Silvie slides her thumb out of her mouth. "I'm dreaming ... I'm dreaming," she whispers. "I'm taking the train to Groningen, and I didn't ask the Nazis for permission first. I'm not scared when the conductor comes in to check my ticket. I'm not a bit scared that he's a German who has come to see if there are Jews on the train. I'm going to Groningen to stay with Grandpa and Grandma de Roos, then with Grandpa and Grandma de Jong, for they haven't yet been sent away to that concentration camp at Westerbork. As the train pulls into the station, I see everyone standing there on the platform. When I jump out of the train, Grandpa de Jong catches me. Everyone kisses me, then we all go together to Grandpa and Grandma de Roos's house. There are cookies on the table, and I get hot chocolate to drink. Grandpa de Roos lets me sit in his lap. He tells me fairy tales, and when he's through, he shells peanuts for me. 'A seven-year-old child is too young to eat unshelled peanuts,' he says. When we're finished eating, we go to the swimming pool. We're allowed to go, because there's no longer a sign there that says FORBIDDEN FOR JEWS. Nice dream, isn't it?"

Silvie climbs out of the chair. "I don't know," she says. "None of it is true, is it? When will we be able to visit Grandpa and Grandma for real? When will we be able to go to the swimming pool again? And I want to go back to my old school *so* much. No, not to that school for Jewish children in the Bezemstraat, but to the other one. I want to be in the same class as Jan and Thijs and Lieneke. And I want to go to school without that yellow star on my chest."

"Me, too," says Rosa. "I've had enough of that rotten star, and I've had enough of those signs that say FORBIDDEN FOR JEWS. Let's close our eyes. If you sit still, the dreams will come automatically. Come here next to me."

Silvie climbs back into the chair. "Put your thumb in your mouth," Rosa whispers. "And close your eyes."

They hear the door open, then the creaking sound of Father's new patent leather shoes.

"Oh, no!" he calls. "Myra, this is terrible. Now *Silvie* is sitting in my chair, too. They're sitting together and sucking their thumbs, without saying a word. It looks as though they're sleeping. They should be running and playing, not sitting in a chair the whole day. Come look, Myra!"

There is the sound of high heels on the steps, then in the living room. Silvie peers at her mother and father through her eyelashes. "It's fun to dream," she says. "I visited our grandpas and grandmas, and I went to the swimming pool. And we still had a radio, too."

Father puts his hands over his ears. "Stop!" he shouts. "I can't stand it! I can't stand this rotten war!"

"But it was fun." Silvie tugs on his shirt. "Come sit with us. And Mama, too. Then the four of us can dream together. What shall we dream?"

"I can't dream anymore," says Father. "Life is one long nightmare. One long, long nightmare."

Mama looks at him. "Stop it, Herman," she says. "You've got to keep your dark thoughts to yourself. I've had enough. You're scaring us all."

Rosa nods.

"That's just the way I am," he whispers. "I've never learned to look at the bright side of things, but I'll try. I don't want to frighten you."

Silvie leans her head against Rosa's shoulder. "Shall we all dream together, then?" she asks. "We'll dream that we're allowed to go anywhere we want. To the park and the zoo and the library. And...and there are no more signs, and no more Germans, either. Is that all right, Rosa?"

Rosa doesn't answer. She's dreaming.

◆ *Fight*

Rosa and Silvie have the nicest aunt and uncle in the entire world. Their names are Lita Rosa and Sander. Lita Rosa is the wife of Papa's brother. Sander is Mama's brother.

Mama always calls Sander "my little brother," for she is ten years older. She has a lot of stories to tell about him. She talks about giving him his bottle, and how he peed all over her when she changed his diapers. One day he scared everyone by saying that he had swallowed a big screw. Sander had such a frightened look on his face that Grandpa and Grandma rushed him to the hospital. When the doctor approached him with a pair of forceps in his hand, Sander shouted that it wasn't true, that it was just a story he had made up. When they were home again, he said that it had been only a very small screw. "It was *so* big," he said, and with his tiny fingers he picked up a grain of sugar to show that the screw had been very small indeed. No one ever did learn whether Sander had told the truth about the screw.

Rosa doesn't think that Sander has changed much since he was little. She considers him to be more like a nice big brother than like a real uncle. He is always telling jokes, even during wartime, and whenever he comes over he cheers up the whole household.

Lita Rosa has almost the same name as Rosa. Her name is Lita Rosa de Jong. Not so very long ago, everyone called her "Aunt Rosa." And Rosa was called "Little Rosa."

By the time she was nine, Rosa didn't want to be called "Little Rosa" anymore. "From now on I'm going to call you by your full name, Lita Rosa," she told her aunt. "I've asked Papa and Mama and Silvie to call you Lita Rosa, too. And *I'll* be just plain Rosa. No more 'Little' before my name."

"Lita Rosa?" Aunt Rosa exclaimed, and she blinked. "What's the matter? Do you mean that I'm not you aunt anymore? Maybe I'll change *your* name, too. I think I'll call you *'Wunderkind.'"*

"*Wunderkind?*"

"Yes, *Wunderkind*. Because you play the violin so beautifully. Are you still taking lessons?"

"Yes. I'm playing a piece by Rieding, and Mrs. Westen says I'm doing fine."

Lita Rosa usually looks splendid. She wears flowered skirts and striped blouses in all sorts of colors: red, green, and purple. She also wears colored bows in her hair: red, purple, and green. She refuses to wear yellow.

Rosa knows that Papa and Mama are embarrassed by the way her aunt dresses. "I want you to look decent tonight. Put your black dress on. And if you insist on wearing a bow in your hair, why must it be such a big one?" Father will say. He wants to turn his sister-in-law into an ordinary woman, but it's no use.

"If you're ashamed of me, just say so. I'll stay home when the rest of your company comes over tonight," she says, and laughs when she sees the startled look on Papa's face.

Rosa often dreams about Lita Rosa and Sander. When she sits in the big chair, she concentrates on them so deeply that they seem to appear automatically. All she has to do is put her thumb into her mouth, and there they are!

"What shall we do today, Rosa?" says her aunt, floating through the room. She is wearing a golden dress and a golden bow in her hair. "Shall we go to Grandpa and Grandma in Groningen? We'll bake cookies for them. And we won't have to take the train. We'll just blow up a balloon, a great big one, and we'll hang underneath it. The wind will take us to Groningen."

"What shall we do today, Rosa?" Sander is in the room, too. He is wearing a silver shirt and silver shoes. "Shall we go to Bilthoven? To the place where we used to go on vacation together? You remember. The house where we stayed was right by a school, and we were allowed to play on the empty playground. I'll come pick you up in my car. The golden one with the diamond roof."

Rosa is growing warm. Whom is she to go with? They're both so nice.

"You're coming with me, aren't you, Rosa?" asks Sander, and he jumps into the air. "See how funny I am?"

"She's coming to Groningen with me," says Lita Rosa, and she pushes Sander away. "See how pretty I am? Look at my hair bow. I'm wearing a golden one today."

"She's coming with me, with me!"

"No, she's coming with me!"

Her aunt and uncle begin to roll on the floor. Lita Rosa's golden dress is starting to tear. A silver shoe flies through the air.

"We'll go together. First in the car, then under the balloon!" Rosa screams.

It's no use. They continue to fight. Rosa can't do a thing about it.

Sander and Lita Rosa finally stop fighting. When they approach Rosa, they each grab her by an arm and begin to pull. She is going to be torn apart!

"No!" she shouts. "I'm not going with you! Go by yourselves. I'm not going!"

"She's at it again." Father's voice reverberates through the room.

"Did you hear what she said?" Mama's voice sounds loud, too. "'I'm not going,' she said. She doesn't want to be sent to Westerbork. That's obvious. And there is nothing we can do to comfort her, poor child."

"If she continues to behave like this, we'll have to get help. A child psychiatrist, perhaps," says Father, and he sighs.

Rosa doesn't move. Her parents don't have to know that they have awakened her. They don't have to know that she has heard everything. Her father and mother are worried about her. And she's glad.

◆ *Back to School*

"Rosa, come on. It's all arranged. You won't be sitting in my chair anymore. You're going back to school."

"Back to school?" says Silvie, and she begins to dance around her father. "Tell us about it!"

"I've gathered together a group of seven Jewish children," Papa explains. "You'll be meeting as a class at the home of Mr. and Mrs. Levie. We've even found a teacher for you. His name is Mr. Rozeboom, and he's Jewish, too, of course, just like the Levies."

"I don't want to go to a Jewish school," says Rosa. "The Nazis made us go to that Jewish school in the Bezemstraat, and I hated it. Each day more and more children were absent because they had been taken away during the night. I was glad when the teacher disappeared, too, because we didn't have to go to school anymore."

Rosa lowers her voice. "Miri says that he went into hiding, and Joel says that he fled to the South of France. I don't want to go to this new school. I'm staying home."

"Nothing doing." Father's voice is loud and angry. "I want you both to go to school. I'm sure you'll like it. Mr. and Mrs. Levie are nice people. They have a little boy named Loetje. You'll probably meet him, too."

"I want to go," says Silvie.

"I don't," Rosa grumbles.

The new school begins today. How fortunate it is that Papa didn't give Rosa's red school bag to Mrs. Bazuin last year. Mrs. Bazuin is their neighbor downstairs. She doesn't have to climb up a flight of steps to reach her living room, as the de Jongs do.

Rosa knows exactly what happened. One evening they were sitting around the table, playing a game. Suddenly, the doorbell rang. Mama turned as white as a sheet, and

Rosa's stomach began to hurt. She always gets a stomachache when something bad is happening.

Papa went to the hallway and opened the door. A woman's voice! They couldn't hear what the woman was saying, but they could hear their father's voice very clearly.

"If you don't get the hell out right away, I'll take this big plant here and throw it down the steps as hard as I can. Now get out!"

They heard Father slam the door. He returned to the living room a bit later. No one dared to ask whom he was shouting at so.

"Leave me alone," he panted. "I've got to get hold of myself." He sat down in a chair, and for five minutes he didn't say a thing. Then he stood up and began to talk.

"Do you know who that was? Mrs. Bazuin. And do you know what she said?"

"No," answered all three at the same time.

"She said...she said..." Papa was practically choking with anger. "She said, 'May I have Rosa's red school bag for Hannie? I heard today that you Jews will no longer be allowed to attend school. May I have the bag? After all, Rosa won't be needing it anymore.'

"And that is why I'm so furious," he continued. "How can she be like that? I don't expect even a little bit of sympathy anymore, but this...I just don't understand."

Father sat down in his chair. He was silent for the rest of the evening.

Rosa has packed her red bag for the first day of their new school. It's full of books and papers, just as it used to be. The address of the school is Juliana van Stolbergstraat

Twenty-nine. The girls want to go by themselves; they are much too old for their mother to bring them.

"Here it is," Silvie calls. "Look, number twenty-nine." She stands on tiptoe and pulls the shiny, polished doorbell.

"Hello." A small, plump woman is standing in the doorway. "You must be Rosa and Silvie de Jong."

"How did you know?" asks Rosa.

The woman begins to laugh. "That's not so difficult. Only single children will be coming now."

"Single children?"

"Yes, children without a brother or sister. And you girls look so much alike that I can tell you're the de Jong sisters. Come in."

She points to the stairway. "The school is upstairs. Mr. Rozeboom is waiting for you. Can you make it? Wait, I'll walk up with you."

They must climb two long flights of stairs. "They're steep, aren't they?" Mrs. Levie says, and she stops for a moment. "I can't climb steps very easily anymore. That's how it is when you're pregnant. A baby is quite a load, let me tell you!" She pats her belly. "Our little son is downstairs, with his father. Later, during your break, the three of us will come upstairs to bring you cookies and punch."

They reach the end of the stairway. "And here is the 'Juliana van Stolberg School,'" Mrs. Levie announces. "That's what we're going to call it. You know, of course, that before the war, this street was called the 'Julianastraat,' after our own Princess Juliana, who is in England now. When the Germans came, they added 'van Stolberg' to her name, because they didn't want a street to be named after a living princess from the House of Orange. That's why our street is now named after a dead princess, instead."

She opens the door to a small room furnished with rows of tables and chairs.

"Well, well, here come two more students," says a small, dark-haired man. He walks up to Rosa and Silvie. "I'm Mr. Rozeboom. Welcome to the class. This is Max, and this is…"

"I already know Max," says Rosa. "He was in my class at the other Jewish school."

"I know Rosa and Silvie, too," says Max. "I thought that you girls had been taken away a long time ago."

"Silly Max," Silvie murmurs.

"Here are your seats," says Mr. Rozeboom, and he pulls up two chairs. "Sit down. And whom do we have here? That must be Jona and Ruth. And there are Mirjam and Jankele. Everyone is here now."

The boys and the two little girls take their seats. They gaze at one another in silence.

"How nice and quiet it is," the teacher continues. "First, I'll need to know what each of you can do. I'll begin with the youngest. The rest of you can read. I have a pile of books on my desk. Help yourselves. And I don't mind if you talk quietly, as long as you don't disturb anyone else."

Mr. Rozeboom sits down next to Ruth. The other children talk and read. "This is much nicer than being at a regular school," says Mirjam.

Mr. Rozeboom confers with each child, one by one. He gives every student some arithmetic problems and a short dictation.

"Good," says Mr. Rozeboom, when he is finished. "Now I know what you can do. And now it's time for our break."

The door opens. A man carrying a tray of cups and glasses enters. A little boy follows him.

"I'm the room father," the man says. "My name is Mr. Levie, and this is Loetje." He points to his son. "Shake hands with everyone, Loetje. And this is my wife. She has cookies for you. May we stay with you during your break? Here, Pien, you take a good chair." He pulls up Mr. Rozeboom's chair for his wife. She sinks down into it, folds her hands over her belly, and sighs.

"It's time for coffee," she says.

"Well, how was it?" Papa inquires, when the girls are home again. "Oh, I see. I don't really have to ask. You both look so happy."

"We had punch to drink," says Silvie.

"We wrote a dictation, and we did arithmetic problems," says Rosa. "And I want to stay at the Juliana van Stolberg School for the rest of the war. Maybe the Germans will stop taking children away now."

Papa peers at Rosa through his glasses. "I hope so," he whispers. "God, child, I certainly hope so."

◆ *List*

Years ago, before the war began, a large picture hung above Rosa's bed. In it were ten farmers, seven women and three men, and when Papa put her to bed in the evening, she would name each one. As he pointed, she would say, "Aunt Eva, Aunt Liny, Uncle Bram, Uncle Marcus, Uncle Izak." Rosa continued in this manner until she had named each person.

Rosa gave each farmer the name of one of Grandma de Roos's brothers and sisters. There were ten children in her family. By the time the youngest was born, the oldest child had already moved out of the house. That is the way it used to be in those days. Everyone is still living except for Uncle Bram, who died before the war. They all settled in Groningen, together with their children and grandchildren.

Many of Grandma's brothers and sisters have been sent to Westerbork. Rosa isn't sure which ones they are, and she doesn't want to know, either.

When the war began, Rosa took the picture down and put it under her bed. When the war is over, she will hang it up again. The picture was replaced with something far more important: a large sheet of paper on which she writes down everything that is forbidden by the Germans.

Rosa is so afraid of doing something wrong that she looks at that piece of paper every night. Imagine what would happen if she accidentally entered the library, or stepped into the park! Such things are forbidden, of course, and that is why Rosa keeps the list above her bed. She has divided the sheet of paper into columns, and has printed dates above them.

1941

May 1:
Jews must turn in their radios.

September 1:

We may no longer go to our own schools, but must attend separate schools.

September 15:
Signs are everywhere: FORBIDDEN FOR JEWS. We may no longer go to the library, to the park, to the swimming pool, and much more.

November 7:
We may no longer change residence. We may no longer travel without permission.

1942

January 1:
We may no longer employ non-Jewish household personnel.

January 23:
We may no longer travel by car.

May 2:
We must wear a yellow star. (Bah!)

May 29:
Jews may no longer go fishing. (Fine for the fish!)

June 5:
We may no longer travel by train, not even with permission from the Germans.

June 12:
We may no longer buy vegetables in non-Jewish stores. We may no longer play sports. (I don't like to play sports, anyway. Fine!)

Rosa must add to her list almost weekly, and she finds it terrible. Won't the Germans *ever* stop bothering them? And on that long list she has written down only the things that are important for Silvie and for her. She hasn't even begun to include the things that the grown-ups must or must not do.

Rosa will be going upstairs soon. She has just learned that beginning June 30, Jews must stay inside their homes from eight in the evening until six in the morning.

She knows exactly why the Nazis have come up with this latest rule. It is easier to track you down and arrest you if you are in your own home. Then all they have to do is check their list and say to one another, "Where is the de Jong family: father, mother, and two children?" A Nazi will run his fat, filthy finger down a typewritten list, and stop when he comes to their names. "Herman de Jong, born September 23, 1901. Myra de Jong-de Roos, born April 6, 1908. Rosa de Jong, born December 13, 1931. Silvie de Jong, born March 28, 1935. They're all Jews, and their address is Broekslootkade Thirty-nine, Rijswijk, South-Holland."

Suddenly Rosa has a stomachache. The pain is so severe that she can hardly sit upright. She doesn't want to be caught. She doesn't want to go to Westerbork.

"What's the matter, Rosa? You're so pale."

"Nothing."

"Something is wrong. I don't think you're feeling well." Mama pulls her into her lap. "Tell me what's bothering you."

"I don't want to go to a work camp. I don't want to go to Westerbork. I can't work. And my stomachache is killing me."

Mama is silent. It looks as though *she* has a stomachache, too.

"Do you know what we'll do, Rosa?" she says at last. "I'll put you to bed with a hot water bottle. That will make you feel better. And when your stomachache is gone, we'll talk some more."

"But I still have something to add to my list. I still have to write about June 30."

"That can wait. It won't be June 30 for a long time. Come on, let's go upstairs."

Rosa walks slowly up the steps. Her hands are clutching her belly.

"I'm right behind you," says her mother. "If you fall, I'll catch you."

Rosa enters her bedroom. When she glances at the paper above her bed, she can see that it looks different than usual. Something has been written in red ink, and she always uses blue.

She stands on her bed and reads what has been printed in bright-red letters:

What we are still allowed to do: sing, read, play the violin, play games, write stories and poems, celebrate birthdays in December, AND MUCH MORE! Greetings and a thousand kisses from your very favorite uncle. Don't be angry with me. Next time I'll use blue ink.

The water bottle is warm, and the bed is nice and soft. Sander is the most wonderful uncle in the whole world. Maybe he is kind of a long-distance magician, for she believes that the red ink is making her stomachache disappear a little.

"How are you feeling now?" asks her mother.

Rosa doesn't answer. She's asleep.

◆ Rhinestone Wedding Anniversary

Rosa and Silvie are standing in the flower shop, hand in hand. At home, everything has been made ready for the big celebration. Together with Papa and Mama they have set up tables and placed chairs around them. The vases in the living room are filled with flowers, and they have set out candles, which they will be lighting soon.

Now they must buy a gift for their parents. The girls have decided to give them a bouquet of wildflowers, poppies and cornflowers and much more. Papa and Mama had wildflowers at their wedding in 1930; surely they will enjoy receiving a bouquet of them tonight.

"Well, young ladies, how can I be of help to you?" says a small man from behind the counter. He is dressed in a yellow coat.

"We want to buy a great big bouquet of wildflowers," says Rosa.

"A great big huge bouquet," adds Silvie.

"Poppies and cornflowers and what else? What did you have in mind?" he asks.

"We'd like every kind of wildflower that you have," answers Rosa, and she lays her red wallet on the counter.

"Do you have enough money?" The man puts his glasses on. "How much do you have?"

"Five guilders," Rosa whispers. "From our own piggy banks."

"You can get some beautiful flowers for that amount. What do you think of this?" He reaches into a bucket and pulls out a bouquet. Water drips down his coat. "Lovely, isn't it? Four guilders and ninety-five cents. You'll even get five cents in change. Why do you want to spend so much on flowers, anyway?"

"We can't tell you," Silvie answers. "We promised Papa and Mama that we wouldn't tell."

"Then don't tell me," he says. "But what would you like? This beautiful bouquet, or something else?"

"This one is fine," says Rosa.

"I like it, too," Silvie adds.

"I'll include a card with the flowers. What do you want me to write on it?" He looks at Rosa. "You tell me what to say, young lady. You're the oldest. How old are you?" he asks, licking the tip of his pen.

"I'm ten and one-half. I'll be eleven exactly six months from today. And I want the card to say, 'For Papa and Mama. From Rosa and Silvie, for their rhinestone wedding anniversary.'"

The man bursts out laughing. "Ha, ha, I've found out, anyway," he says, and begins to write. His lips are turning purple, for he is licking the tip of the pen after each word.

Suddenly he stops. "*What* did you say?" He lets his glasses slide to the tip of his nose. "Rhinestone wedding anniversary? Never heard of it. How long have they been married?"

"Twelve years."

"Twelve years? *Rhinestone?* I've been in the flower business for years, and I've never heard of a rhinestone anniversary. Strange, very strange. They're playing a joke on you, young ladies."

He looks at the yellow stars on their dresses. "Oh, now I understand," he exclaims. "It's a Jewish tradition, of course. We Dutch people don't know too much about those things."

"*We're* Dutch, too," says Rosa. "Our great-great-great-great-grandparents lived here."

"Oh, yes, I thought so..." he says, and continues to write. "There. Finished."

"May we leave now?" Silvie is already standing by the door.

"You still have to pay me, girls. Remember? Four guilders and ninety-five cents. And I hope you have a very fine day. Here are the flowers. They're heavy, aren't they? And with the change you can buy two licorice drops. To celebrate your parents' rhinestone wedding anniversary."

"Run!" Silvie shouts as they approach their house. "Sander is already there. His bicycle is in front of the door."

"Not so fast. The flowers are heavy," says Rosa. She stops for a moment, for she has a pain in her side. "You go ahead," she pants. "I'll be there in a minute."

"Hello, my little nieces!" calls Sander from the top of the steps. "Come on up. What do you have there, Rosa? What beautiful flowers! What are they for?"

"Should we tell Sander?" Rosa whispers to her sister. She stands on tiptoe. "Papa and Mama are celebrating their rhinestone wedding anniversary tonight," she whispers in his ear.

"Well, well," Sander whispers back to her. "How interesting. I know that today is their twelfth anniversary. I myself was present at the ceremony. I was a little boy then, but I remember everything. Did you say *rhinestone*? Oh, well, I don't know much about these things. I'm just an old bachelor. Ow, don't tickle me, Silvie. Be serious for a moment. Why don't you take those flowers to your room? Then you can officially present them to your parents this evening. I've heard that a lot of visitors will be coming."

"It's a shame that our grandpas and grandmas can't come," says Silvie. "They should be allowed to leave Westerbork for a rhinestone anniversary, shouldn't they, Sander?"

Their uncle looks very unhappy. "Grandpa and Grandma de Roos and Grandpa and Grandma de Jong will certainly be thinking of us, even though they're in Westerbork. I'm sure they'll remember that today is your parents' twelfth anniversary. But travel? No, they're not allowed to do that. Don't cry, sweetheart." He takes a large handkerchief and wipes the tears from Silvie's cheeks.

"Don't cry," he repeats. "We must see to it that the bride and groom have a festive evening. Agreed? Let's shake to that."

Silvie shakes her uncle's hand.

"Good," he says. "Now take the flowers upstairs right away. And put on your very best dresses."

When the girls come downstairs in the evening, the living room is full of people.

"Lita Rosa!" Silvie shouts, and she jumps into her aunt's lap.

"Mr. Nuszbaum!" Rosa greets their neighbor with a handshake and a kiss.

"Do you know how old I am?" he asks. "I'm...I'm... sometimes I forget how old I am."

"You're eighty-six years old," says Mama. Mr. Nuszbaum lets go of Rosa's hand.

"Uncle Jossie, Aunt Lenie!" The children don't know whom to kiss first, for so many friends and relatives are present.

Not everyone is able to attend the celebration, however; that's just not possible anymore.

There are coffee and tea to drink, and butter cake to eat. The candles are burning brightly, and everyone seems to be talking at once. The house hasn't felt this cozy in a long time. It is best not to think about her grandpas and grandmas in Westerbork. What would they be doing now? Rosa shakes her head very hard. Perhaps all her unhappy thoughts will disappear then.

"Dear people, may I say a few words?" Papa is standing next to his chair. "Please be quiet for a moment." He turns toward his brother-in-law. "You, too, Sander. Do you think that this is just an ordinary gathering tonight? Well, it isn't. We have invited you because Myra and I wanted to celebrate our rhinestone wedding anniversary. You've probably never heard of it, have you? Well, we haven't, either, because a rhinestone anniversary doesn't exist. We made it up ourselves. Actually, we should be inviting you six months from now, for our copper anniversary. But we didn't want to wait so long because, dear people, who knows where we'll all be then? The times are so uncertain."

"Long live the rhinestone anniversary couple!" Sander calls, and he raises a piece of butter cake high above his head. "Cheers!" he adds.

"The flowers. I'll go get the flowers!" Silvie runs out of the room.

"Long shall we live," Mr. Nuszbaum sings. "And may we remain neighbors for a long time to come. In glory!"

"Wait a minute." Father tries to gain everyone's attention. "There is another important reason for inviting you this evening," he continues, and turns toward Rosa.

"Our Rosa will celebrate her eleventh birthday exactly six months from today," he says, still looking at his daughter. "And I repeat: Who knows where we'll all be then? What will the Nazis have in store for us? That's why, dear people, Myra and I have decided to celebrate Rosa's birthday today." He reaches for a package. "And here, my big girl, is the gift that Mama and I bought for you." He walks toward Rosa.

"No!" she screams. "No!" She runs out of the living room, and bumps into Silvie in the hallway. The bouquet falls to the floor.

"The flowers!" Silvie shouts. "You're stepping on the flowers. Look, they're all over the place!"

Rosa rushes into the bathroom and locks the door. She sits down on the toilet and begins to cry. She doesn't want to celebrate her birthday, not yet. She was born in December, and she has always celebrated her birthday in December. She doesn't want to celebrate it again until six months from now, when it is time to do so. And as far as she is concerned, her parents can keep the gift. She never wants to come out of the bathroom again. Let the grown-ups all go to hell with their celebration.

Rosa grabs the end of the roll of toilet paper and begins to pull. The mound of paper on the floor grows higher and higher.

"Rosa! Open the door." Sander's voice.

She doesn't answer.

"Rosa, listen to me. I can understand that you think it's strange to be celebrating your birthday now. *I* think it's strange, too, but let's not ruin the evening. Come on, sweetheart, we'll play some music together. All right? That nice piece for violin and piano that we've been practicing. Remember?

"No!"

"Of course you remember. That piece by Mozart. You can play it better than I can."

"No!"

"Shall I tell them that you don't want to celebrate your birthday now?"

"Yes."

She hears Sander's footsteps in the hall. It seems as though all the guests have left. The only sound she hears is her uncle's voice. Slowly she unlocks the bathroom door.

"Come on," says Sander. "I can see that the door is already open a little. Come with me. You don't have to celebrate your birthday now." He puts his arm around her shoulder. Together they walk into the living room.

"May I have your attention?" Sander taps a cake fork against a coffee cup. "You've all noticed how upset Rosa is to have to celebrate her birthday now. And she's right to be upset. Children are often wiser than we adults are. So this is what we'll do: Exactly six months from today we'll gather here to celebrate Rosa's eleventh birthday. Let's hope that we'll all be present on December 13, 1942. Here, in this house. It will be a celebration for everyone who is here now, and for all those who were not able to come today. Agreed, Herman?"

Father doesn't answer.

"Agreed, Herman?" Sander repeats in a loud voice.

"Agreed," Father whispers. He stares at his black patent leather shoes, not daring to look at anyone.

"Long shall we live!" Mr. Nuszbaum calls. "And may we remain neighbors for a long time to come. No one is going to take *me* away, for I like it very much here in Berlin..."

"That's where he was born," Father whispers. "He can't remember things very well anymore. He's not suffering, though."

"Long shall we live," Mr. Nuszbaum repeats. "And may we remain neighbors—"

"In glory!" the grown-ups shout. "Hip, hip, hooray!"

◆ *Psychic*

Papa is sitting in the big chair with his hands over his eyes, mumbling to himself. Rosa, Silvie, and Mama are already at the table. On each plate is a serving of meat, potatoes, and applesauce.

"We're next," they hear their father mutter. "What can Mr. Nuszbaum possibly do in a work camp? If they're hauling away people as old as he is, they'll certainly be coming for us younger people, too. That poor fellow doesn't even know where he lives some of the time. Twice I've had to bring him home because he was out wandering the streets. When I went to check on him this morning, I found out..."

"Shall I tell you a story about Sander?" Mama doesn't wait for an answer. She begins to talk very fast. Her voice is so loud that they can no longer hear their father at all.

"One afternoon Sander told Grandma de Roos that he was 'going to kick a ball around.' Grandma looked at him in surprise, for not long before he had stated that he was never, ever going to play soccer again. He was about eight years old at the time. He had played on a soccer team for a couple of weeks, but before long he had had enough of it. He would pick flowers growing along the side of the field, and would forget that he was supposed to be kicking the ball, just like all the other little boys on the team. But Sander thought that picking flowers was much more fun. 'Soccer, ugh,' he said, and whenever he was supposed to play, he would develop all sorts of ailments: headache, sore throat, vomiting. Finally, Grandpa and Grandma let him quit the team. That's why Grandma was so surprised when one Wednesday afternoon, Sander announced that he was 'going to kick a ball around.'

" 'I thought that you never wanted to play soccer again,' she said.

" 'But I want to play this afternoon,' he answered. 'And now I'm going to get dressed.'

"He appeared a few minutes later wearing his black soccer shorts, red sweater, and a purple cap on his head.

" 'I do believe you're going to perform in a circus,' Grandma told him. 'You look like a little clown.'

" 'See you later!' Sander shouted.

" 'Have a good time!' Grandma called. 'And remember, be home in time for supper!'

"Late that afternoon, Grandma decided to return some library books, for otherwise she would have to pay a fine. I went with her, and we walked arm in arm together. As we were nearing the library, we saw Sander. How far from home he was! Why? With one hand he was clutching his soccer ball to his chest. We couldn't see what he was doing with his other hand; we were still a bit too far away, but we could see that he was bringing his hand to his mouth.

"We walked a little further. 'Would you look at that,' Grandma said, and she let go of my arm. 'That young man is smoking. Unbelievable.'

"Great clouds of smoke were coming from Sander's mouth. I wanted to run up to him and take the cigarette away, but Grandma held me back.

"'Just wait,' she said. 'I'll get him. You stay out of this.'

"At supper that evening, Grandma asked, 'Well, Sander, how was your afternoon? Did you have a good time playing soccer?'

"'I'll say,' Sander didn't even bat an eye.

"'So, whom did you play with?'

"'With…with…uh…Hennie.'

"'A girl?'

"'Yes…no…a boy. What's the matter, Mother? You're acting so strange.'

"'Oh, it's nothing, nothing at all. I'm just sniffing a little.'

"Grandma stood up and began to smell Sander. He blushed, and started to rock in his chair. Grandma kept sniffing. Sander began to wolf down his potatoes, shoveling them into his mouth again and again.

"'Did you know that I've become a psychic?' Grandma asked, all of a sudden. 'I can see what people have been

31

doing, even though I wasn't with them at the time. Shall I give you an example? I'll try it with you first, Myra.'

"Grandma looked directly at me, then closed her eyes. 'You went...you went...you went to the library this afternoon. Am I right?'

"I hardly dared to look at her, but I nodded.

"'Good. So I was right. Now your turn, Sander,' she said, walking over to him. She looked deep into his eyes. 'Keep looking at me,' she whispered. 'Sander de Roos, you played soccer.'

"'Yes,' he said with a sigh, and he looked very happy.

"'*You*, Sander de Roos, did something else. I see...I see...clouds of smoke...a cigarette. *You* have been smoking, one cigarette, at the least.'

"'No!' Sander was nearly in tears.

"'Yes!' Grandma exclaimed. 'I can see it now. You were clutching your soccer ball to your chest, and smoking at the same time. I can see it right before my very eyes.'

"'I'll never do it again,' Sander whispered. 'Never again.'

"I didn't dare look at Grandma. I couldn't help laughing, yet at the same time I felt sorry for Sander. I'm sure he told his friends how awful and scary it was that his mother was psychic, and could see what he was doing, even though she wasn't there with him. Later, much later, we told him that Grandma had actually seen him smoking that Wednesday afternoon. Fortunately, he thought it was very funny, and had a good laugh about it."

Mama looks at Papa, who is hunched over in his chair. "Do you know that story?" she asks.

"Story? What story?" Papa sits up a little, and places his hands on the arms of the chair.

"The story I just told about Sander."

"I wasn't listening." He buries his face in his hands once again. "Poor old Mr. Nuszbaum," he says softly. "He fled from Germany in nineteen thirty-eight, only to be captured in Holland four years later. But perhaps there is one comfort. If he didn't know where he was when he was living here in Rijswijk, maybe at Westerbork and in Poland he won't have any idea at all."

"Poland?" Rosa asks, and rises from her chair.

"Sit down, Rosa," says her mother. "And please come to the table right away, Herman. For God's sake, come to the table. Stop talking about Mr. Nuszbaum. It makes me so sad."

"It makes me sad, too," says Rosa.

"It makes me want to cry," Silvie whispers.

Slowly Papa walks to the table. They begin to eat as soon as he is seated.

Cold potatoes with meat and applesauce.

◆ Oh, So Sad

Each Monday morning before school, Rosa and Silvie must wash the breakfast dishes for their mother, who has a choir practice to attend. The director of the choir is Samuel Primo, and the name of the group is *Sheer Ha'shalom*.

"What a crazy name," Silvie remarked on the first Monday. "Why is it called 'Sheer?' Sheer, sheer, do you want some beer?" she joked.

33

"'*Sheer Ha'shalom*' is Hebrew, and it means 'Song of Peace,' their mother explained. "And our group is made up entirely of Jewish women."

Mama looks happy when she returns from the rehearsals. "We're singing a very beautiful oratorio," she told her family. "It's called 'Elijah,' and it was written by Felix Mendelsohn-Bartholdy. As soon as we've learned it thoroughly, we're going to perform it. You will all be invited to the concert, and I'll want you to listen carefully to my favorite song. It's about Jews who are suffering and who have no one to comfort them."

"How sad," Silvie exclaimed. "How sad for those Jews."

Monday morning. Mama is at choir practice. Papa is reading *The Jewish Weekly*. Rosa and Silvie are sitting in the big chair. They don't have school today because Mr. Rozeboom is sick.

"What do you think Mama is singing now?" Silvie asks. "Maybe she's singing about the Jews who have no one to comfort them." She runs a fingernail through the plush arm of the chair.

"She's been gone for a long time," she continues. "I wish that she were home. I hope she hasn't been caught..."

They hear the sound of the key in the door. "Mama!" The girls run to the hallway.

Their mother doesn't answer. She brushes past them. "Wait right here," she says.

"Has someone else been taken away?" Silvie asks.

Mama doesn't hear her. She steps into the living room, then returns to the hall. "Come on," she says, taking off her raincoat. "I'll tell you what's happening."

The girls return to the big chair. Father is seated at the table, leaning on his elbow. "Tell us, Myra," he says.

Mama clears her throat. "A half hour ago, when I was coming home from choir practice, I met a woman on the street, a woman I'd met at Lita Rosa's and Jossie's house. I thought she was very nice then, and I liked the way she spoke with such a delightful French accent. When I asked how she was doing, she began to cry. I felt terrible, of course, and asked her what was wrong.

"'Tomorrow we must move out of our house,' she sobbed. 'The Germans will be taking it over. And we don't have to go to Westerbork yet. According to my husband, we've been given a deferment because we're from France. The Germans aren't deporting any French Jews, for the time being. But I have to find a place to live now. What are we going to do? It's so terrible for our little Philippe.'

"I tried to comfort her. I asked her if she had been to see Lita Rosa and Jossie. 'No,' she said, 'I couldn't. They have only two rooms themselves. The three of us can't impose on them like that.'

"I promised her that I would discuss the situation with Papa and you, and now I'm asking if they could move in with us for a while. What do you think?" She looks at Papa. "We don't have much time to decide."

"I want to help these people," he says. "What happened to them could have happened to us, too. We'll take them in, even though it will be very crowded here. This is only a temporary arrangement, however; they'll have to try to find someplace else to live. But I don't mind if they stay with us for the time being."

Mama showers him with kisses. "You're a dear," she says. Papa looks embarrassed.

Silvie tugs on her mother's sweater. "Who is little Philippe?" she asks. "How old is he?"

"Don't ask me now," Mama answers. "First I want to hear what you and Rosa think about it. And then I'll have to go to the family right away."

"But first we need to know how old Philippe is," says Rosa.

"Philippe is thirteen months old. He is—"

"Wonderful!" Rosa exclaims. "That's wonderful!"

"We're going to get a little brother, a little baby brother!" Silvie shouts. "Oh, what fun!" She dances around the room.

"Shhh, you'll disturb Mrs. Bazuin," their mother warns. "I'll go see the Mendes family now." She puts her raincoat back on. "See you later!"

Mama is already down the stairs.

◆ Mon Petit Philippe

Together with their father, Rosa and Silvie move a white crib into their bedroom. Papa places a small blue blanket inside.

"Both of you used to sleep under this," he says, and he strokes the blanket. "We didn't think we would ever be using our crib again."

The girls' beds have been pushed together. "It looks like a grown-ups' bed," Silvie remarks. "Just like a bed for a father and mother."

Rosa has climbed on a chair to re-hang her list above her bed. The picture of the farmers is now hanging above the crib.

"I hope Papa doesn't start naming all the people at bedtime again," she says to Silvie. "Uncle Marcus has been taken away, and so has Aunt Eva. I don't want to think about that before I go to sleep."

"I don't, either," Silvie answers. "It makes my eyes water."

"There they are! I can hear them downstairs," says Rosa, and she jumps off the chair.

The girls rush down the steps. Before entering the living room, they nearly collide into a highchair and an easel in the hallway.

A man and a woman with a baby in her arms are standing in the room. The woman walks toward Rosa and Silvie and offers them her hand. "I'm Isabelle Mendes," she says, "and this is my husband, Louis. And this..."

"Ta, ta," says the baby.

"...is Philippe, *mon petit Philippe*."

"How sweet. May I hold him?" asks Rosa.

"No," says Silvie, "*I* want to hold him."

"Oh, oh," says Father.

"We'll put Philippe down on the floor," says Mr. Mendes, and he reaches toward his son. "Come to Papa, Philippe."

"Pfff," says the baby. Bubbles spill out of his mouth.

"Rosa and Silvie will watch Philippe while I show you up to your bedroom in the attic," says Mama. "It's not very big. That's why I hope you don't mind if Philippe sleeps with the girls in their room. I'm sure that they will be very quiet, and that they will take good care of him."

"Whatever you decide is all right with us," Mr. Mendes answers. "We're refugees now. I just hope that I can paint a bit while I'm here. I'm an artist by profession. Oh, well, when you're a refugee..."

"You mustn't say that," Papa admonishes him. "You are not a refugee to us. I hope that you feel at home here. And you wife and your little son, too."

"Thank you, Mr. de Jong. Thank you very much." He takes Papa's hand.

"Don't." Papa pulls his hand away. "You don't have to thank me. And please call me Herman."

"Call me Silvie," says Silvie, and she giggles. "And you can call my sister 'Rosa,' because that's her name. We're Silvie and Rosa de Jong." She runs out of the room.

"What are you doing?" her father calls to her. "Come back!"

Silvie returns to the living room. "I'm going outside and I'm going to yell to everyone that I have a little brother. And I'm going to yell out his name, too. Philippe...Philippe Mendes."

"People won't believe you if you say that," says Rosa. "A real brother would be named de Jong."

"No...oh, no...If they don't believe me, then I'll just say that his name is de Jong. Philippe de Jong." Silvie dashes out again.

Mama turns to their new houseguests. "Would you like some tea?" she asks. "And what does the baby drink?"

As they relax and drink their tea, they can hear Silvie shouting outside.

"His name is Philippe! *Mon petit Philippe* de Jong!"

◆ *East*

Rosa and her mother are finally alone in the house. She doesn't know where everyone else has gone, and she doesn't care, either. Rosa tries to play the piece by Rieding, but it isn't going very well today. Later, when her mother comes downstairs, she will have something to ask her, something important. Actually, it is a question that she doesn't dare ask, but she is going to, anyway.

Rosa lays her violin on the table, and sits down in the big chair. She can hear the sound of heels tapping against the floor above her as her mother walks from the bedroom to the hall, then down the steps. The door to the living room opens.

"Why aren't you doing anything?" says her mother, standing by the chair.

"I'm doing something."

"I don't see anything."

"You can't see what I'm doing. We have to go to Poland, don't we?"

"Rosa!" Mama sits down in a chair across from her. She folds her hands in her lap and looks directly at her daughter.

"Mama." Rosa takes her mother's hand. "Please say something."

"What am I supposed to say?"

"Say that we have to go to Poland. Is it true? A little while ago Papa said that Mr. Nuszbaum had to go to Poland, and that the Germans would be coming to get us, too."

Mama nods. Now Rosa knows that it is true.

"How did you find out, Mama?"

"Do you really want to know?"

"Yes."

"Then come with me." Mama lifts her out of the chair. "You're getting heavy," she says. "Take my hand."

They walk toward the dining room cabinet. Mama climbs on a chair, and gropes for something inside the cabinet.

"Here it is," her mother whispers. She has a postcard in her hand.

"Come down from the chair," Rosa says, and she reaches out to help. Mama leans on her, and climbs slowly down.

"This is how we know," says her mother, and she waves the card. "Shall I read it for you, or will you...?"

"Give it to me." Rosa wants to take the card, yet at the same time she is afraid to do so. When she suddenly has it in her hand, she can see that it isn't a postcard at all, but a photo. She recognizes the people in the picture, doesn't she? She stares at it for a long time, and then she knows. How could she not have realized it sooner? It is Uncle Ies and Aunt Dien de Jong and their children, Clary and Freddy. Clary is a little older than she is, and Freddy is a bit younger. They look different from the way they did a year ago, which was the last time they were all together. They all have had their hair cropped short in this photo; Clary has, too, and she used to have such beautiful long braids. It is obvious from the picture that Clary's breasts have begun to develop. Aunt Dien and Uncle Ies look serious, Clary is smiling, and Freddy is sticking out his tongue. Uncle Ies has placed his hand on Clary's shoulder, and Aunt Dien is resting her hand on Freddy's head. "Westerbork, July 1942. Dien, Ies, and children. Life was nicer in the Justus van Effenstraat Eleven, Utrecht," is written in a white space underneath.

"Turn it over," Mama whispers.

Rosa studies the back. It looks like a postcard, for pencil lines have been drawn, and a stamp has been placed on it. She reads the writing, then reads it again, but doesn't understand what it says. Perhaps all the dreaming has made her forget how to read all of a sudden.

"Give it to me," says her mother.

Rosa hands her the photo. Mama begins to read. "'To the H. de Jong Family. Broeksloot…'"

"I know that. I read the address myself. Read the other side of the pencil line, Mama."

"Don't be angry, sweetheart."

"I'm *not* angry. Now read."

"'Just time enough to send you this photo. In half an hour we're going east, to Poland, they say. We're strong. The children won't have to work, thank God. We'll all pull through this together. We're fine, and hope you are, too. So long. Dien, Ies, and children.'" She gives the picture to Rosa.

Rosa stands in silence as she looks at the picture again. She takes her handkerchief and wipes a speck of mud from Clary's face.

"We didn't want to tell you yet. But now you know. Terrible, isn't it, Rosa? We're all so unhappy, but we didn't want to trouble you and Silvie with our sorrow. You girls already have enough troubles to bear."

"I won't tell Silvie," Rosa says, and she turns over the picture. "There's something else written in red pencil."

"Read it," says Mama, wiping the tears from her cheeks.

"'To the finder of this photo,'" Rosa says. "'Will you please put a stamp on it and mail it for us? We can't, because the train is ready to take us to Poland. We'll try to throw this card from the train. Thank you, and God bless you.'"

"Come here, sweetheart." Mama sits down and pulls Rosa onto her lap. They hold each other, and cry so hard that they can barely stop.

"Look what I've done to you," says Mama. "I should have told you that we don't have to go to Poland. Maybe that would have been better."

"Papa already said that we do. Besides, you shouldn't lie to me."

Rosa's eyes are still full of tears, but they are no longer streaming down her cheeks. "Maybe Freddy is happy now," she says. "He'll no longer have to look for the watertight pan with holes at the bottom."

They begin to laugh, softly at first, then a bit louder.

"Rosa, every time Freddy came over, Papa would tell him, 'Fred, my boy, I need the watertight pan with holes at the bottom. Go look for it. I think it's in the linen closet.' Freddy didn't understand that your father was just playing a joke on him. I can still see him looking for the watertight pan with holes at the bottom. Poor Freddy." Mama sighs deeply.

Rosa sighs, too. Even though she has put the photo back into its place, she feels that it is very close; the letters seems to be stabbing her right through the cabinet.

Mama is still seated. "Shall we eat?" she asks.

"I don't think that God is going to bless us," says Rosa.

"What do you mean?"

"They asked on the photo to bless only the person who found the card. They wrote 'God bless you' in those red letters."

"Then *we'll* ask God to bless us," Mama whispers. "Shall we do it now, or would you rather wait until you go to bed?"

Mama walks into the living room, and sits down in the big chair. "Come sit in my lap again," she says. "I think that you would rather talk to God now."

Rosa curls up in her mother's lap. Mama holds her stiffly in her arms. "You begin," she says to her daughter.

Rosa closes her eyes. "*Baruch ata Adonai*...No, I think I'll say it in Dutch. Maybe God understands Dutch better then Hebrew."

"Go ahead." Does Mama have tears on her cheeks again?

"Dear God. Will you please bless us, too? We're related to Aunt Dien and Uncle Ies and the children in the photo. We didn't find the photo. Someone else did, someone we don't know. But will you bless us, anyway? Thank you, God. Oh, yes, bless Aunt Dien and Uncle Ies and Clary and Freddy, too. In case you didn't know, God, they're in Poland now. But the children don't have to work, thank goodness. They have very short hair, God. All four of them. But you already know that, because Grandpa de Roos says that you know everything. Amen."
Rosa opens her eyes.

"Amen," Mama whispers. "Thank you for your prayer." She is still holding Rosa close to her.

Very close.

◆ Mr. Rieding

Before Aunt Isabelle, Uncle Louis, and Philippe came to live with the de Jongs, the piano was hardly ever touched. Mama had lessons a long time ago, but she never plays anymore. Before the war, Papa played all sorts of songs from memory. Now that it is wartime, he no longer feels like playing.

"We should sell the piano," he said, but Mama didn't want to do that. It's a good thing, too, for Uncle Louis can play the piano beautifully. He plays happy songs, and whether you want to or not, when you've heard those tunes a couple of times, you can't help singing along. He plays pieces like "Folks, Dare To Live" and "Look for the Sun."

Those songs cheer everyone up except for Papa. "It's easy to say," he growls. "'Folks, Dare To Live.' In these times. Not to mention 'Look for the Sun.'"

Sometimes Rosa tries to play along on her violin, but she doesn't like the way it sounds very much. She plays a different kind of music for her violin lessons, music that was written long before the popular tunes were. She practices a lot, and her teacher, Mrs. Westen, is satisfied with her progress.

"If you practice a little harder, you may play that piece by Rieding with me on August nineteenth," her teacher has said. "I'm having a student recital here in my house. I'll accompany you on the piano. You've had lessons for over three years now, and I think that you're ready to play before an audience. Performing in a recital is a lot of fun. You'll have a chance to hear the other students, and they'll have a chance to hear you, as well. All the parents will be invited, and grandparents, too."

Rosa practices her piece every day. Sometimes Uncle Louis plays with her, using no music at all. They sound wonderful together.

"If Mr. Rieding could hear us, he would be clapping hard," Uncle Louis says.

Rosa can imagine a man wearing a long white coat. His hands are pale and thin, and he can't clap very hard, of course, because he has been dead for years. But she can hear him clapping, anyway.

Where did that Mr. Rieding live? She must ask Mrs. Westen about it.

"We'll play the Rieding one more time," says Mrs. Westen. "And we already have an audience. Look." She points to her children, Marnix and Carina, who are sitting quietly on the floor.

"You must now tell your audience the name of the piece we're going to play," Mrs. Westen continues. "I'll say it first. It's called 'Concertino in Ungarischer Weise Opus Twenty-one, by Rieding.' Now it's your turn. Go ahead."

"Ladies and gentlemen," Rosa begins. "We're going to play 'Concertino in...in...on a Hungarian Tune Opus Twenty-one, by Rieding, and...'"

"What's an opus?" asks Carina.

"*Opus* simply means a work," Mrs. Westen explains. "It is the twenty-first work by Rieding. You announced it very well, Rosa. But you must also say 'boys and girls,' not just 'ladies and gentlemen.'"

After Rosa announces the piece again, Marnix and Carina clap as hard as they can. Rosa and her teacher begin to play.

"Bravo!" calls Mr. Westen, who has entered the room very quietly. "Bravo! That was absolutely beautiful. What a wonderful recital it's going to be! I'm already looking forward to it."

When Rosa returns from her violin lesson, she tells her family all about what happened. "The recital will be on August nineteen," she says, "and Mrs. Westen is going to let me perform with her."

"What did you say?" asks Father, looking at her. He puts his newspaper down. "When is that recital?"

"August nineteen."

"You should keep in mind that by August nineteen, it's possible that the Germans will no longer allow us to visit the homes of non-Jews," he warns. "You know yourself that they're always coming up with new rules to make our lives miserable."

Rosa is so startled by her father's words that she can hardly talk. It feels as though she has a big piece of apple caught in her throat.

"Then...can...I might not be able to play in the recital. That's mean! If I can't go to Mrs. Westen's house, I'll never play the violin again. Never! That's so mean."

"What's mean, Rosa?" Uncle Louis asks, entering the room.

"I might not get to play in the recital."

"Why not? What are you talking about?"

"Papa thinks that by August nineteen, we might not be able to go to the homes of non-Jews. And this is the first time in my life that I'd be allowed to perform before an audience, with Mrs. Westen."

It is dead still in the room. No one moves at all. Rosa

can think only about Mr. Rieding in his long white coat. How terrible it is that she might not be allowed to play before a real audience. It seems that every time she turns around, there is something else that the Germans won't let her do.

"I have an idea!" says Mama, jumping out of her chair. "I know of a way that would enable you to play in the recital for sure."

"What do you have in mind?" Papa asks, and he puts his cigar in the ashtray. "I'm waiting. Tell me."

"It's very simple." Mama's cheeks are flushed, all of a sudden. "Maybe you're being too pessimistic again; that's just the way you are. But even though there hasn't been anything about it in the newspaper yet, you may be right. That's why I think it would be better to invite everyone to come *here* for the recital."

"They'll never come." Rosa is nearly in tears. "A while ago, Martha was afraid to even talk to me. Do you think that she would dare to come to our house?"

"Then Martha won't come," her mother says. "Just wait. I'll take care of everything." She walks into the living room, and picks up the telephone.

"Hello, this is Mrs. de Jong," is all that Rosa hears, for her mother has closed the sliding glass doors. Through the doors they can see her from the back, bending over the telephone. She turns around. Her hands are playing with the telephone cord. She looks at the people in the dining room, smiles, then hangs the phone back up on the wall.

Mama opens the doors. "It's all arranged!" she exclaims. "Everyone will be coming to our house on the nineteenth of August. That's what Mrs. Westen thinks, at least. We'll provide the cookies and punch. And when you're no longer allowed to go to Mrs. Westen's house, she will come *here* and teach you."

"Long live Opus Twenty-one by Rieding!" Uncle Louis calls. "Long live the Concertino in Ungarischer Weise. Composed years and years ago, and now played in a Jewish home. Aren't you happy, Rosa?"

"I guess so," she whispers.

"How quiet you are. Why is that?" Uncle Louis asks, and he pulls her onto his lap. "What's wrong, my little violinist?"

"What are we going to do?"

"What do you mean?"

"What are we going to do if the Nazis say that non-Jews may no longer come to our house? I know for sure it's going to happen."

"Sweetheart." Uncle Louis pats her on the cheek. "Do you know what we'll do then?"

"No."

"You'll play, anyway, and I'll accompany you. You know I can play that piece from memory. We'll invite all the Jews of the whole city to come listen. Shall we do that?"

"All right."

"And we'll make posters," Silvie exclaims. "We'll hang them up all over the city. And we'll write on them: *Concert by Rosa de Jong and Louis Mendes on August 19, 1942. They will play a concertino by Rieding called 'A Hungarian Tune.'*

"And do you know what else I'll write on the posters? I'll put... I'll put... something really mean."

"What?" Rosa is very curious. "Tell me."

"Now don't be angry, Papa." Silvie doesn't look at her father. "At the bottom of the posters I'll write in bright-red letters: FORBIDDEN FOR NON-JEWS."

◆ Bathroom

Rosa and Silvie must get used to the fact that Aunt Isabelle and Uncle Louis sometimes go naked when they walk from their bedroom to the bathroom.

At first, Rosa wanted to warn Aunt Isabelle. "Look out! You're completely naked. Everyone can see you," she wanted to say, but now she is glad that she kept quiet. Because Aunt Isabelle and Uncle Louis believe that it is normal to go without clothes, Rosa now considers it to be normal, too. She thinks that she will try it herself one day. Perhaps it feels good to go around in your bare skin. And if she walked naked through the house, everyone would see that her breasts are beginning to develop a little, just as Clary's are. Rosa is very proud of her breasts. She is glad that she is not a boy. Boys remain flat-chested their entire lives. How boring that would be!

Even though Aunt Isabelle isn't ashamed of being seen nude, she locks the bathroom door every now and then. Silvie has noticed it, too.

"What could she be doing in there?" she has asked Rosa. "Why does she lock the bathroom door some of the time, when at other times she isn't ashamed of walking around in her birthday suit?"

Rosa doesn't know, either. She is very curious about Aunt Isabelle, just like Silvie. "If she should forget to lock the door sometime, I'll just walk in 'by mistake,'" Rosa promises her sister.

"Psst, Silvie. Come quickly. There she is!" says Rosa, pointing to the bathroom. "And the door isn't locked. I'm going in now."

Rosa opens the door very slowly. Aunt Isabelle is standing in front of the sink, completely dressed.

"Rosa, what are *you* doing in here?" she asks, holding her hand over her mouth. "What? You, too, Silvie?" she says, keeping her mouth covered.

"I'll bet you have false teeth," Silvie exclaims, "and you don't want us to know. That's why you always keep the bathroom door locked."

Aunt Isabelle bursts out laughing. Rosa blushes.

"Can the two of you keep a secret?" Aunt Isabelle asks.

"Yes," they answer.

"Let's lock the door first." Aunt Isabelle closes the door. "Look at what I'm doing," she says, and she picks up a brown bottle. "What is written on the label? You read it, Rosa. The words are difficult."

"Hydrogen peroxide nine percent," Rosa says.

"Right. And what am I going to do with it? Watch carefully," Aunt Isabelle says, and she takes a wad of cotton. Her voice keeps getting softer. "I'm going to put a little of that stuff on this wad, and smear it under my nose," she explains.

"Under your nose?" Rosa looks wide-eyed at Aunt Isabelle. "What's the matter? Do you have a cold?"

"No, I don't have a cold. And now for my secret: I have a little mustache, and I find it embarrassing. But if the mustache is blond, you can barely see it. That's why I bleach it with peroxide. Now make sure you don't tell anyone. Louis doesn't even know about it. I keep the bottle hidden in here." She puts the peroxide back into the medicine cabinet, which hangs above the sink.

"Don't come near it," she warns the girls. "This stuff is very dangerous for children."

"Come on, let's get going," Silvie says to Rosa. She turns to Aunt Isabelle. "We just thought that you were doing something weird," she says.

In bed that evening, the girls discuss Aunt Isabelle's secret. They must talk quietly, for they don't want to awaken Philippe. They are glad to know what is going on behind the bathroom door; at least they no longer have to suffer from curiosity now!

"Do you want to have a blond mustache someday?" Silvie whispers.

"I want to have a blond mustache *now*, and blond hair, too," Rosa whispers back. "The Germans like you much better if you're blond."

"Shall we..." Silvie stops abruptly.

"Shall we what?"

"Shall we go into the bathroom and turn our hair blond with the stuff from that bottle?"

"Are you crazy?" Rosa is no longer whispering. "Aunt Isabelle said that stuff is very dangerous for children."

"I'm going, anyway." Silvie has already climbed out of bed. "I want to be blond."

"Then I'll go with you. Don't put your slippers on. We don't want anyone to hear us."

The girls sneak down the stairs. Fortunately, Philippe is still sleeping. In the living room, one floor below, the grown-ups are talking so loudly that they surely cannot hear the creaking of the steps.

They walk into the bathroom. "I'll lift you up so that you can get the bottle." Rosa tries to pick up her sister, but Silvie slips to the floor. They begin to laugh.

"We'll try again," Rosa whispers. "Quick, grab it!"

Suddenly, Silvie has the brown bottle in her hand. "Hurry and get the cotton," she says.

They help each other, for they know that they must work rapidly.

"Shut your eyes," Rosa whispers. "It mustn't get in your eyes."

The peroxide bubbles and foams so noisily that it sounds as though it is singing a song. When the girls have finished, the bottle is empty.

"We'll put the bottle back in the cabinet," says Rosa. "And if we leave the cork off, they'll think that the stuff has evaporated."

"Ouch, it stings," Silvie whispers.

"I'll blow on your head," says Rosa, "and then you can blow on mine."

They creep quietly back upstairs. Philippe is still sleeping. His thumb is in his mouth. Rosa kisses him on the hand.

"I hope he still likes us tomorrow, when we're blond," says Silvie.

"Of course he'll still like us," says Rosa. "Babies don't notice things like that."

When Rosa awakens the next morning, she looks at the other bed. Does Silvie have a new stuffed animal? A red stuffed animal is lying on her pillow. Rosa reaches out to grab it.

"Ouch, get your hands out of my hair! Don't pull it. You're hurting me. Why are you…" Silvie looks at her sister with wide eyes. "Your hair is bright red!" she shouts. "Our hair turned bright red! Mine did, too."

"Yes, yours did, too."

"What are we going to say? Now everyone will know what we've done. What are we going to do?" Silvie begins to cry.

"We'll say…we'll say…that last night…I don't know what we're going to say," Rosa answers.

"We'll say that we didn't want to have black hair any longer, and that we liked red hair better. And then they can figure out for themselves how we did it, and—"

"Aren't you awake yet? Are you still…" Their mother is standing in the room. Her eyes shift from Rosa to Silvie, then back to Rosa again.

"*What's this?* What have you done? Your hair is bright red!"

"We wanted blond hair," Rosa whispers. "We wanted to have beautiful blond hair."

"And so we used hydrogen nine percent," Silvie explains in a loud voice.

"Oh, no." Mama sits down on Silvie's bed. "This will never do," she says. "I'll have to cut your hair very short. Don't go downstairs yet. I'll go first, and prepare Papa for the shock. Otherwise you'll scare him half to death. And don't expect people to recognize you with your red hair."

"I don't care," says Rosa. "I don't play outside, anyway."

"I do," says Silvie. "Then the other children will finally have something funny to say to me. Then they'll call:

> *Lighthouse without a light,*
> *A rotten face, red eyes so bright.*

"And I think that's funny."

"You think that's *funny?*" Mama looks at Silvie in surprise.

"Oh, yes." Silvie stands next to her bed. "It's much funnier than that other rhyme they usually yell to me:

> *Jew in a moat,*
> *Fall out of your boat,*
> *Sink all the way down,*
> *And drown.*

"I'm going downstairs," says their mother. "I can't stand listening to those awful verses."

◆ *Cleaning Woman*

"I can't take it anymore, Herman," says Mother, and she sighs. "With so many people in the house, I've just got to have some more help. Isabelle sits around and reads French books the whole day, and Louis does nothing except copy pictures. And he calls that art."

"But they're very nice people," says Rosa.

"*Very* nice," Silvie echoes, and she jumps from one leg to the other. "Very, very nice, especially *mon petit Philippe*. He is a sweetheart."

"Stop that," Rosa says. Silvie's restless behavior bothers her, for their mother already looks so tired and unhappy.

"I can help you, can't I?" Rosa says to Mama. "Mr. Rozeboom is still sick, and probably won't be back for a while. I can wash dishes and mop floors and…"

"And what else can you do, little maid?"

No one heard Sander enter the room. "What's the matter?" he asks. "You all look so glum. Come, tell me." He sits down and rests his feet on the table. "Tell me what's wrong."

"I can't take it anymore." Mama is nearly in tears. "All these people around me. All this sorrow."

"Do you want Isabelle and Louis and their sweet little son to leave?" Sander asks. He rises and puts his hand on Mama's shoulder.

"No, of course not. Where would they go? I want to have a cleaning woman again. I want one just as nice as our Laura, whom we had to let go because the Nazis no longer allowed her to work for us."

Laura. Rosa sighs when she thinks about her. Laura was such a dear. She often brought Rosa and Silvie to her home, which she shared with Jannes, her fiancé. The four of them would play Monopoly, Parcheesi, and other games. It was very cozy at their house.

There was something strange about Laura's eyes. She was unable to look directly at you. Her eyes continually moved from side to side, the whole day long. Rosa wondered if her eyes also moved at night, while she slept. On the very day that Rosa had finally gathered enough courage to ask Laura about it, it was too late; the young woman was no longer working for the de Jongs because the Germans had forbidden it.

Rosa's thoughts are interrupted by the sound of her uncle's voice. She jumps.

"Don't laugh," he calls loudly. "I'll make sure that you get some new help. Everything will be all right by tomorrow."

"How?" asks their mother, and she looks at Sander in disbelief. "How old is she? What's her name? You know that the girl will have to be Jewish, don't you?"

"Didn't I just say that things would work out? Put your trust in Sander, and everything will be okay. Wait and see. I'm leaving now, because I have some drawing to do in my studio. I'm working on an advertising poster, to be used after the war. But first I'm going to get you your new household help."

"I'll be curious to see what happens," says Mother.

"Me, too," says Father, and he sighs.

The doorbell rings at eight o'clock the next morning.

"I get to open the door!" Rosa shouts, and she runs to the steps. She is terribly curious about their new cleaning woman. She pulls on the string that is hanging by the top of the stairs, and opens the door. She sees a mass of red hair, then a broom, and another broom. Rosa still cannot see the person's face.

"May I come up?" a deep voice asks.

"Of course. Come upstairs," Rosa answers. She steps back to allow the girl enough room to pass through with her brooms. The girl is walking very slowly. Perhaps it is scary to begin working in a new household.

They are upstairs now.

"I'm Rosa." Rosa extends her hand.

"And I'm Bram," is the answer, "but you can call me Brammetje." It's a man who's squeezing her hand. "Well, well, isn't that funny? Your hair is just as red as mine. But mine is natural, of course," he says, still squeezing her hand.

"Mama!" she calls. "Come quickly!"

"Where can I begin?" Bram has set the brooms against the bathroom door. "Here?"

He reaches into a bag and takes out an apron. "Nice apron, isn't it?" he says.

"Stop…What…what kind of…" Mother is so nervous that she can hardly speak.

"Shall we go into the living room? Brammetje would rather talk when he's sitting comfortably in a chair."

Mother and Rosa follow him into the living room.

Bram walks straight toward Father. "I'm Brammetje, your new household help." He pumps Father's hand.

Father grimaces. "I'm pleased to meet you, sir," he says.

"Yes, I thought as much. My name is Bram, but you can call me Brammetje."

Father puts his hands in his pockets.

"We had asked for a girl," says Mother.

"Why, for God's sake?" Bram looks at her in surprise. Then he turns to Father. "Women certainly can be stupid, don't you think? They don't believe that we men can work."

"Hm," Father mutters.

"Actually, I'm a hairdresser by profession, but ach, you know what the times are like. We're no longer allowed to have non-Jewish customers, and alas, there aren't many Jewish customers left anymore." He sighs deeply. "I thought: come, Brammetje, you must make yourself useful. So I reported to the Jewish employment agency, applied for a housekeeping position, and here I am! I'd like to begin cleaning now. And later on I'd like a nice cup of coffee, please. Around ten o'clock or so," he says, and he walks out of the room.

Rosa looks at her parents, and notices that they are having difficulty suppressing their laughter. If only they would laugh out loud! It's been such a long time since they have done that.

They can hear Bram singing in the hallway: "Two eyes so blue, two eyes so blue."

The vacuum cleaner hums, the buckets clatter, and now and then Bram has a question to ask. "Where is the copper polish? Do you have some cleanser?"

Each time he enters the living room, Father and Mother can barely keep from laughing.

"Are you a real cleaning woman?" Silvie asks.

"No," Bram answers. "Do you know what I am? I'm... I'm...a cleaning *man*."

Silvie bursts out laughing. The rest of the family laughs, too. It is all right to laugh when a person is actually *trying* to be funny.

"Oh, my, what a relief," says Father. He is laughing so hard that his eyes are full of tears. He takes his handkerchief and wipes them away. "I can't hold it in any longer. What a splendid figure he is."

"Shall I make some coffee? It's already ten o'clock," says Brammetje, standing in the doorway. He doesn't wait for an answer. Fifteen minutes later he returns with a serving tray laden with cups.

"I've warmed some milk for the children," he says. "Come to the table, everyone!"

"We always drink our coffee on the sofa," Rosa wants to say, but she remains silent. Everyone must do what Bram says today.

"I've made delicious coffee." Brammetje wraps both hands around his cup and drinks noisily. "Delicious," he repeats.

"When are you coming back, Bram?" asks Mother.

"I thought I'd come three days a week. I've heard that other people are living here with you. Where are they?"

"They're still in bed," Father explains. "Artists, you understand. They always sleep late."

Mother glares at Father.

"Even their little boy sleeps late," Father adds.

"Stop it, Herman." Mother is angry now. "It's bad enough that they have no home of their own."

"I thought I'd come three days a week," Brammetje continues. "But you've got to keep one thing in mind. A day may come when I'm no longer able to work for you."

"We're well aware of that," says Father, and he sighs.

"No, it's not what you think. Brammetje isn't going to be dragged out of his house. The Germans had better watch out! Brammetje is a very good fighter. No, they won't be taking Brammetje away. If Brammetje doesn't come, it means that something else is at hand."

He is speaking so softly now that Rosa can barely hear him.

"If Brammetje doesn't come, it means that he's fighting for the Allies. There will be an invasion soon, an attack.

The Russians, Canadians, and Americans will come help us. And Brammetje will be helping, too." He looks at everyone.

"Brammetje will come rescue all of you. I'm not only handy with clippers and scissors, I'm handy with a gun, too."

He stands up, and pretends to hold a gun in his hands. "Pow-pow-pow...Here is Brammetje. Watch out, you Nazis. Here I come!"

He sits down again. "Shall I get to the beds now?" he asks, looking at Mother.

"Fine," she replies. "Not the beds of our guests, but you know that. You can do theirs on the day after tomorrow."

"As long as I don't have to fight," he promises, and leaves the room.

From their places in the living room, the de Jongs can hear sounds of great importance above them. Brammetje is working.

"You'll never have to lift a finger again," Father exclaims. "Look at what that man can do!"

"Finished." An hour later Bram is standing in the living room. He takes off his apron. "She's pretty," he comments.

"What are you talking about?" asks Father.

"I'm talking about that woman upstairs. I believe her name is Isabel. That's what I heard someone call her, at least."

"That's right," says Father. Rosa notices that he is blushing.

"Her name is *Isabelle*," Papa explains. "I-sa-bel-le. Pretty name, isn't it? It's French."

"I know," says Bram a bit angrily. "Many of my hair products had French names."

60

"I'm sorry," Father apologizes. "I hadn't thought about that."

"Well, I'm leaving now," says Brammetje. He doesn't move.

"Well, I'm leaving now," he repeats. "Even though I don't like going back to an empty house. My parents were taken away last week, you see. I wasn't home at the time. I wanted to follow them, but I don't think it would do any good. They may be dead already, there in those work camps. We don't know the fine details, do we?"

"Stay with us," Mother urges. "We have room for you here."

"No, absolutely not." Bram walks toward the door. "When the invasion comes, they'll need to know where I am. They'll need to find me at home. Goodbye, everyone! See you later!"

Bram strides out of the room. They can hear his footsteps on the stairs.

Mother runs to the hallway. "Don't forget your brooms, Brammetje!" she calls.

"I'm leaving them here!" he shouts. "If the good Lord is willing, I'll be back to use them on the day after tomorrow."

◆ Dates

"Let's practice again, Silvie. What were we no longer allowed to do on November seventh, nineteen forty-one?"

"I don't want to," Silvie whines. "I want to sleep."

"No." Rosa is growing impatient. "It's much too hot to sleep. We've got to go over these dates."

"All right." Silvie sits up in bed. "I'll tell you about all the things that Jews aren't allowed to do," she begins. "November seventh, nineteen forty-one: they may no longer travel without permission, and may no longer change residence without permission."

"Good, you get an A! And what about September fifteenth, nineteen forty-one?"

"They may no longer stay in non-Jewish hotels, or go to theaters, libraries, or swimming pools. It's a shame that we aren't allowed to go to a swimming pool, isn't it, Rosa? It's so hot now."

"Keep going," says Rose sternly. "We're going over dates. What happened on May second, nineteen forty-two? You should know this one, because it wasn't that long ago."

"I know it!" Silvie raises her voice. "It's a difficult word: *introduction* of the Jewish star. All Jews from the age of six years are required to wear the Jewish star, which must be clearly visible on their clothes."

"How did you learn all those difficult words?" Rosa looks at her sister in astonishment.

"Silly, don't you know? I read *The Jewish Weekly*. I read the difficult words over and over again, until I can say them from memory. Lucky, isn't it?"

"Lucky? What's lucky?"

"It's lucky that I learned to read when I was in kindergarten. The teacher used those crazy letters made from sandpaper. She would blindfold me, and I'd have to feel the letters, and say what they were. It was kind of scary."

"One more date," says Rosa. "What happened on May twenty-ninth, nineteen forty-two?"

Silvie begins to roar with laughter. She is so loud that Rosa begins to laugh, too.

"May...twenty...ninth...I can't stop laughing," Silvie gasps. She rolls out of bed, and lands on the floor with a thud. Rosa falls down next to her. They are laughing so hard that tears are streaming down their cheeks.

"Quiet!" calls a voice from below. "If you don't stop that noise, you're really going to get it!"

"Then we're really going to get it!" Rosa shrieks. "We know what we're going to get, don't we?"

"Mama will come upstairs and give us a good hard spanking," Silvie answers. "My bottom is much fatter than yours. A spanking will hurt you much more than it will hurt me."

"You're mean!" says Rosa, and she gives her sister a push. "You shouldn't say that. As if I can help being so skinny. You are a big fat pig. I have a nice little song for you!" She sings:

> Have you ever heard about
> That Hollebolle-wagon,
> Where that Hollebolle Gijs sat
> And stuffed his little face?

"Ouch!" Rosa says. "Don't hit me. We don't want to awaken Philippe." She tries to keep Silvie's hands away. "Stop it. Oh, no, here comes Mama."

The girls jump into their beds. "Quick, get your pillow!" Silvie calls.

When their mother enters the room, they are lying quietly with their eyes closed.

"You two aren't sleeping," says Mama.

"Yes, we are!" Silvie whispers. "Look, my eyes are shut."

"Turn over, both of you. I'm going to give you a spanking." Mama pulls their covers away. "One, two," she calls.

"Three!" the girls shout.

Mama's hand lands on Silvie's bottom. "Darn!" she exclaims. They burst out laughing.

"I *knew* you'd do that," says their mother. She is practically choking with laughter. "I knew that you would put pillows in your pajama bottoms. But settle down now, please. We would like to have some peace and quiet."

"We were reciting dates," Silvie explains, "and we started to fight."

"Dates? Shall I quiz you, Rosa?"

"Okay!"

"Let's begin. I think that this is still a bit too difficult for you, Silvie."

"It is not," Silvie protests, and she blushes. "I knew them all."

"Let me think. All right, here is the first question," says their mother. "When was Bonifacius killed at the Battle of Dokkum?"

"In seven fifty-four!" Rosa calls.

"And when was the Battle of Nieuwpoort? Your turn, Silvie."

"I don't know," Silvie whispers. "I haven't learned about those kinds of dates yet. Shall I quiz *you*, Mama?"

"All right, but I'm not very good in history. Go ahead, though."

Silvie sits up in bed. "What were the Jews no longer allowed to do on November seventh, nineteen forty-one?" she asks solemnly.

"We were no longer allowed to travel, and no longer allowed to change residence," Mama answers quietly.

"Right," Silvie exclaims, satisfied. "Jews were no longer allowed to travel or to change residence without permission. Next question: What were the Jews no longer allowed to do on November twenty-first, nineteen forty-one?"

"Stop!" says Mama, and she puts her hands over her ears. "Stop it, for God's sake. How terrible it is that you have to learn these dates."

"We've learned them well, haven't we, Mama?" says Silvie. She kisses her mother on her forehead. "One more date," she continues. "A very, very funny one. What were the Jews no longer allowed to do on May twenty-ninth, nineteen forty-two?"

The girls are laughing so hard that they are rolling on the floor again.

"What's the matter with you?" asks their mother. "I do believe you've lost your minds!"

"I'll tell you." Rosa stands next to her bed. "On May twenty-ninth, nineteen forty-two, the German authorities decided that Jews may no longer…"

"Fish!" Silvie shouts. "Plaice, herring, smelt, have no fear! You no longer need to be afraid of Jews. Jews may no longer do anything anymore. They may no longer visit non-Jews. They may do their shopping only between three and five o'clock. But I don't think Rosa has put that down on her list yet."

"Go to sleep now," says Mama. "The world can revolve

without you. Take your pillows out of your pajamas, and sweet dreams."

"I'll dream about plaice and herring and Jews." Silvie is almost asleep. "And...about...Dok-kum."

"Goodnight, Mama. Look at Silvie. She's already sleeping."

"Goodnight, sweetheart. Maybe you'll have a new date to learn soon: August or September, nineteen forty-two. Holland is liberated from the Germans. Jewish children are allowed to live normal lives once again. They may go to the library, to an ordinary school, to the swimming pool, and—"

"Do you really think that will happen?" Rosa pulls her mother's head down close, and showers her with kisses.

"I hope so," Mama replies.

"I hope so, too," says Rosa.

◆ *Figaro*

Rosa glances at the clock. It is already nine in the morning. Brammetje said that he would be coming "the day after tomorrow." The day has arrived, but he isn't here yet. Where could he be? His brooms are in the hall, where he left them. Uncle Louis and Philippe are so curious about Bram that they have awakened early to see him.

The doorbell rings at ten o'clock.

"Brammetje!" Rosa runs to the steps, and opens the door.

"I'm a little bit late, aren't I? That's because I had so much equipment to scrape together." Brammetje trudges up the steps. "It's heavy, too. But I'm here, thank goodness." He sets a pink suitcase down in the hall.

"Where are you going to begin, Brammetje?" asks Mama.

Brammetje thinks deeply before answering. "I'd like to begin here, in the living room," he says. "That seems to be a very suitable place."

"You already know where your things are. I put them away in—".

"My things are in here." Brammetje walks to the hall, and returns with the pink suitcase. "Here are my things," he says, slapping the suitcase.

"Are your mops and brooms in that case?" asks Rosa.

"Mops and brooms?" Brammetje looks at Rosa as though she has lost her mind. "Who said anything about mops and brooms? We're going to do something else first. I'm going to give everyone a haircut this morning. I've reserved the afternoon for household work."

Bram opens the suitcase, and takes out all kinds of bottles and tubes. He lays three pair of scissors down on the buffet.

"Who wants to be first?" He has a cotton cloth in his hand. He shakes it out. "No hair. Good. You are a very tidy hairdresser, Bram."

Rosa doesn't dare look at Mama. She is afraid that her mother is going to laugh at Bram for talking to himself.

"Who, then? I don't have all day."

The door opens. Bram turns around, and stares silently at Aunt Isabelle, who has entered the room.

"You are even more beautiful than you were two days ago," he whispers. "If you would take a seat, please, I'll give you a haircut."

"Fine," says Aunt Isabelle, and she laughs. "I was told that you are a hairdresser. I've had enough of this long hair of mine."

Brammetje ties the cloth around Isabelle's neck, making a large knot at the back. He takes scissors and begins to snip. Aunt Isabelle's curls fall to the carpet.

"I'll clean the hair up myself," he says. "That's the advantage of being a hairdresser *and* household help, too." He gestures in a stately manner as he dances around Isabelle.

"You are just like Figaro, the barber from the opera *The Barber of Seville*," she comments.

"Figaro...Figaro...Figarooooooh," Brammetje sings. "You're all aware that I'm not just a simple hairdresser, aren't you? When the war is over, I'll go to Paris, to learn more about my profession. And in Paris I'll come to you, Madame Isabelle, for French lessons."

"*D'accord*. Am I finished now? I've got to go upstairs, to Philippe."

"Does your little boy have any hair yet?" asks Brammetje hopefully.

"Not very much."

"That's too bad, for I'd like to have given him a haircut, too. And you don't have to pay, of course. This Figaro wants to keep up his skills a little bit. If he doesn't, when the war is over, he won't know how to cut hair anymore."

Bram looks at his watch. "Goodness gracious, it's already eleven o'clock. It's time for you to make some coffee, Mrs. de Jong. And I'll start cutting Rosa's hair now. You are finished, Madame Isabelle. Have a look." He takes a mirror from the suitcase.

"Is that really me? I look like a little boy," she says, making a face at the mirror.

"Yes, but a *beautiful* little boy," says Brammetje. "I hope that madame is satisfied."

"It's a shame that we can no longer go out," says Aunt Isabelle. "When your hair looks this nice, you should go dancing."

"You'll be able to do that in a little while," Brammetje says. "They've told you about the invasion, haven't they? I'm expecting it to come at any moment."

"Invasion?"

"Yes. In a couple of weeks you'll be able to go out dancing again. The Allies will soon be here to liberate us, and Brammetje will be fighting with them. Ask Mrs. de Jong if you want to know more about it. I've explained the whole plan to her, and I have neither the time nor the desire to talk about the invasion again, and about how Brammetje will be fighting with the Allies, and—"

"Be careful, Brammetje," says Aunt Isabelle softly.

"Brammetje isn't crazy. Brammetje isn't going to die for a long time. Next! Your turn, Rosa."

"Mama cut my hair just a little while ago, and Silvie's hair, too. When our hair turned red, all of a sudden."

"That doesn't matter. Sit down. I promised to give everyone a haircut, and that includes you, too."

"Well, well, do you all look absolutely stunning, or not?" Brammetje gazes around in satisfaction. He has taken his scissors to everyone; only Philippe's hair remains unchanged.

"Paris has nothing on me," he says, beaming. "I give a first-class haircut. And now I'll get down to work. No, I won't. I'll have something to eat first. I'm so hungry I could faint. Aren't you going to eat?"

"We don't set the table at lunchtime," Mama explains. "We have a sandwich on the run."

"Wrong. Wrong! Listen to Brammetje. You must never do that. As long as you're together, you must do everything possible to make things cozy. No more sandwiches on the run. Set a proper table and sit down together. I can see that no one ever has to eat alone here. I know what it's like to put your plate on your lap and gulp your food off of it. Rosa, you set the table. For eight people. Philippe will be eating, too."

Silvie begins to giggle.

"Don't you dare laugh at me," Brammetje threatens. "If you do, I'll never cut your hair again."

"The brooms, the chamois, and the vacuum cleaner. Who will fetch them for me? I'd better get down to work now. I've had enough to eat. Thank you for that extraordinary lunch." Brammetje rises, and bows to Mama and Aunt Isabelle.

"I'll begin here in this room, for there is still hair on the floor from this morning," he says.

"I was just about to sit down in my chair and read the newspaper," Father grumbles.

"That's too bad. Brammetje must begin his household work now. You can read your paper this evening. As for the rest of you," he says, pointing to the others, "go outside or something. It's a beautiful day. Be happy that you can still go outdoors. Now get out of my room."

They do as Brammetje says once again. Rosa and Silvie go to their room. Papa goes outdoors with Mama and Aunt

Isabelle. Uncle Louis says that he is going to paint in the kitchen.

"All right, Mr. Mendes, but later on you'll have to go somewhere else with your mess, because I have to clean the kitchen. Philippe may stay with me. I'll let him ride on the vacuum cleaner in a little while."

When they return to the living room an hour and a half later, Bram is at work upstairs. Smells of furniture polish and bleach fill the house.

Brammetje sings: "I love Holland...Figaro...Figaroooooh."

"Finished. It's five o'clock already. I've got to go." He is standing in the hallway with the pink suitcase in his hand.

"See you Friday, Brammetje."

"If I don't have to fight," he promises. "You never can tell. And the Allies can't win without Brammetje. Brammetje will be back again on Friday, at nine o'clock sharp."

"If the good Lord is willing," says Aunt Isabelle.

Friday:

Rosa doesn't understand it at all. It is already quarter past nine, and Brammetje isn't here yet. He couldn't be fighting now, could he?

The doorbell rings at twenty minutes past nine. Could that be Brammetje?

Rosa runs to the hall, and pulls on the string. The door opens slowly. A woman is standing downstairs.

"Is this the de Jong household? I'm from the Jewish employment agency, and I have some information about

Brammetje. Brammetje can't come, and you surely know the reason why." She looks at Rosa, then turns around, blowing her nose loudly. The door slams behind her.

"Brammetje can't come today," Rosa tells her family. "And he can't come tomorrow, or the day after tomorrow, either. Brammetje has to fight."

"Poor Brammetje," says Mama softly. "Poor red-headed Brammetje."

◆ Rosa Stops Playing

"Come on, Rosa," says Sander, kneeling before her. "Get your violin out and play something. You haven't touched your instrument for such a long time."

Rosa doesn't answer. She leans her head against the back of the chair. She doesn't want to look at Sander. She doesn't feel like playing the violin anymore. Mrs. Westen can no longer come to her house to give her lessons, because not long ago she broke her leg while climbing onto a step stool. And the Germans won't allow Rosa to go to Mrs. Westen's house anymore. Papa was right when he predicted that Jews would not be permitted to visit the homes of non-Jews.

Rosa imagines what it might be like if the Germans still allowed her to go to Mrs. Westen's house. She would stand next to her bed and play beautiful melodies. Perhaps her teacher's leg would heal faster then. "Rosa," Mrs. Westen would say, "you are the smartest doctor in the whole world.

Play that piece by Joseph Fiocco now. When I'm feeling better, I'll accompany you on the piano."

"Rosa." Sander lays his hand on her head. "If you wait too long, your fingers will become so stiff that you won't be able to play at all."

"I don't care." Rosa turns her back to her uncle. "Leave me alone," she snaps.

"Shall I tell you a story?"

Rosa turns around a bit. "No."

"How silly of you. I was going to tell you about old Sandor Rosevici, who traveled from village to village playing his violin, and—"

"Sandor Rosevici. Who is that?" Rosa peers at Sander over her shoulder.

"He was...he was...Rosa, let *me* sit in the chair. You come sit on my lap, and I'll tell you all about Sandor Rosevici and his family."

Rosa slides out of the chair very slowly.

Sander takes her place. "Come on," he says. "Come up on my lap, and listen carefully. Listen to the story of the Rosevici family.

"Long ago in Russia, there lived a father, a mother, and six children. There were three boys and three girls, and all of them could play a musical instrument. Each child played more beautifully than the next, and they were often invited to perform at wedding celebrations. How wonderful the violins, flutes, drums, and harmonica sounded! They traveled from village to village. At first they went on foot, but when they had earned enough money, they bought a horse and wagon. Thus Sandor Rosevici and his family earned a living as they wandered from village to village, from city to city.

73

And their work brought them great happiness. They spent their nights at various inns, and sometimes people enjoyed their merry music so much that they invited the family to sleep in their homes.

"Everything was going well until one fateful day, when the mayor of a village called Proyzeck prohibited them from making music there. He didn't even allow them to stay in his village. The mayor of Proyzeck was a proper gentleman, you see, and he didn't like people who had no home of their own, and who traveled by horse and wagon from one place to another. And the mayor of the next village was a proper gentleman, too. All the mayors were proper gentlemen. The Rosevicis were forbidden to make music everywhere they went, and this caused the family great sorrow.

"So they crossed the border of that inhospitable land, and they crossed other borders, too, until they came to Holland. Upon their arrival, they brought out their flutes, violins, and other instruments, and began to play beautiful music once again. They played at the village markets and squares, and everyone stopped to listen. Some people had tears in their eyes, especially when Marjanka, the youngest daughter, played her violin. There was a piece in which you could hear her quite well because the other instruments played very softly with her. It was a tune about their distant land. When Marjanka played it, all the sounds of the market stopped; you heard only Marjanka playing her violin. Her father, mother, brothers, and sisters hummed along."

"What kind of tune was it?" asks Rosa.

Sander doesn't answer. He is not looking at Rosa, for his eyes are closed.

"One day, when Marjanka was playing the tune, a gentleman approached her. He was a tall man dressed in a long black coat, and he was carrying a cane with him. He stood near Marjanka, and swayed to the beat of the music.

"The song ended, and he began to clap. When he pulled off his white gloves, the clapping grew louder. 'Bravo!' he cried. 'Bravissimo!' He called out much more, too, but no one in the Rosevici family understood what he was saying. Finally, one of the bystanders went to fetch Mr. Kiwalski, the shoemaker. Mr. Kiwalski was a foreigner, but he had lived in Holland for a long time. Perhaps he was from the same country as the Rosevicis, and could tell them what the stately gentleman was saying. And apparently he *was* from the same country, for he and Sandor Rosevici spoke the same language.

"'This gentleman here is very impressed with your daughter's playing,' Mr. Kiwalski said. 'He is asking whom she studies with.'

"Mr. Rosevici answered.

"'She doesn't study with anyone,' Mr. Kiwalski translated. 'The girl's father says that no one in the family has had lessons because they move around so much.'

"The stately gentleman shook his head. 'Ask if I may be her teacher. I'll come to her house and give her lessons.'

"Mr. Kiwalski spoke very rapidly to Sandor Rosevici, and Sandor Rosevici replied.

"'They have no house. They wander throughout the land,' Mr. Kiwalski explained.

"'Then I'll give them a house and I'll...'

"Mr. Kiwalski stepped back. 'Now I see!' he exclaimed. 'You are...you are Giovanni Colesi, the famous violinist!'

"The stately gentleman nodded. Mr. Kiwalski fell to the ground, and kissed the legs of his trousers.

"'Oh, get up,' said Mr. Colesi. 'I don't like that kind of overblown attention. I'm a good violinist, and I'm going to take that family under my wing.'"

"Well, did it happen?" asks Rosa. She is enjoying the story so much that she is blushing with pleasure. "Did Mr. Colesi do what he had promised?"

"Of course. Marjanka became world famous. The Rosevicis were even allowed to perform for the king. And they never had to wander from village to village again. From then on, their horse pulled the king's coach, and the animal became a favorite of the princes and princesses. The Rosevici children were allowed to go in and out of the royal palace as they pleased. But there was one thing that the family found rather unpleasant: The king asked them to change their name. He thought that since the Rosevicis felt so at home in Holland, and since they spoke Dutch so well, they should have a Dutch name, too. And what did their name become? What do you think, Rosa?"

"How am I supposed to know?"

"You can figure it out. Think hard."

"I *am* thinking hard, but I really don't know."

"What is my name?"

"Sander de Roos."

"Say it again, Rosa. Slowly, please. Say it slowly."

"San-der de Roos."

"Don't you hear anything?"

"San…Sandor…Rosevici. I hear it! You have the same name, except yours is in Dutch."

"Right. And Grandpa and Grandma de Roos, and your

mother, too. Our name is actually Rosevici, and…we are extremely musical. Our talent comes from our famous ancestors. I'm named for Marjanka's father. And that's why I want you to keep playing. You mustn't give up the violin, not when you have such renowned ancestors. Will you please keep playing, Rosa?" Sander lays his head against her cheek.

"You'll stay with it, Rosa. You are a descendant of the Rosevicis. You must never forget that. And later, when you become a well-known violinist yourself, you'll take the name of our famous ancestors. It's a very musical name. Listen: *Rosa Rosevici.*"

"I'm not promising anything," says Rosa.

"What an impudent girl you are," exclaims Sander, and he laughs. "You should be a bit more polite to your old Uncle Sandor Rosevici."

◆ *Philippe Cries*

Rosa and Silvie often have trouble falling asleep because Philippe cries so much. They try to comfort him, but they aren't always successful.

"He's having trouble teething, *mon petit Philippe*," says Aunt Isabelle.

"He's a nervous baby. He can sense that we're not very happy these days," says Mama.

Rosa finds it horrible when Mama says such things. She wants *so* much for her mother to be happy, but it is difficult to be happy in these times. People are continually being taken away. Already there are four women missing from Mama's choir. One day they were singing about Jews who needed to be comforted, and the next day they were in a work camp. That is why the entire household is unhappy—Philippe, too.

It's happening again. The girls have been in bed for an hour, and Philippe won't stop howling.

"It's driving me crazy," says Silvie. "Stop it, Philippe!"

Philippe cries even louder. Rosa has been lying with her head under her pillow. She comes out from underneath. Her face is bright red. "Whew, it's much too hot for that," she puffs. "Watch out, Philippe. If you don't stop crying, I'll put my pillow over *your* head. Then we won't be able to hear you anymore."

Philippe is quiet. "It was just a joke!" Rosa calls. "I wouldn't ever do that to you."

Philippe begins to cry again. His mouth is open so wide that the back of his throat is visible.

"Why don't Aunt Isabelle and Uncle Louis come to check on him?" Silvie grumbles.

"The four of them are sitting on the sofa with their arms around each other and cracking jokes, of course," answers Rosa, and she giggles. "When grown-ups are busy doing things like that, they don't pay attention to children. And then *we* can't sleep. Shall we take him into bed with us?"

"That would be fun." Silvie is already standing next to the crib. She reaches out to Philippe. "Come on," she says.

Philippe raises his arms up to Silvie. She lifts him out of the crib.

"Careful!" Rosa cries. "Don't let him fall!"

They place Philippe between them. He puts his thumb in his mouth and gazes first at Rosa, then at Silvie. He slips his thumb out of his mouth, and begins to laugh.

"A little mouse comes walking by," Rosa sings. "Tickle, tickle, tickle."

Philippe chortles.

"We're going to sleep now," Rosa tells him.

"Ta, ta," says Philippe.

Rosa feels something on her face. Is it a mosquito? She slaps it away.

She tries to rub the sleep from her eyes. Who could be crying so loudly? It's Philippe. How did he get into her bed? At first Rosa doesn't understand what is happening. Then she remembers that Silvie took him out of his crib. Surely Philippe is crying because she has rolled over on him and has crushed him. She takes him in her lap, but the crying doesn't stop.

Silvie is awake, too. "What's the matter with Philippe?" she asks.

"I think I've squashed him. I rolled over on him while I was asleep.

"How awful." Silvie strokes his head. "Did she squash you, Philippe?" she asks in a mournful voice.

Philippe cries even harder.

"He stinks," says Silvie. "He's not squashed, he's dirty. Shall we change his diaper?"

"All right," says Rosa, and she fetches a clean diaper from the cupboard.

Silvie removes the dirty diaper. "Disgusting," she says. "Bah, my hands are full of poop. I've got to wash my hands!" She runs to the sink.

"Hold him!" Rosa shouts, but it is too late. Philippe rolls off the bed. He lies on the floor, motionless, not making a sound.

"He's dead!" Silvie shouts. "Look at him!"

Philippe begins to cry as he has never cried before. He waves his arms and kicks his legs.

"Be quiet." Rosa takes him in her arms, and strokes his belly. "Shhh, quit now."

"We'll never do anything so stupid again," Silvie whispers. "Here is a clean diaper for you."

Philippe begins to smile.

"We've got to clean him up first," says Rosa. She lays Philippe down on her bed, takes a washcloth, and wets it at the sink. "Come here with your bottom," she says, laughing. She grasps him by his feet, raises him up, and slaps the washcloth against him. Philippe begins to shriek. He is crying so hard that he is turning blue.

They hear footsteps on the stairs. It is Uncle Louis.

"What is going on here?" he asks.

Silvie starts to cry. "We let him fall," she sobs.

Uncle Louis speaks very softly to Philippe. "Shhh. I'll sing you a song. But first let's make sure that you're all right." He undresses his son, and feels his little body carefully. He tickles him under his chin. Philippe is still crying.

"I think he's all right," says Uncle Louis.

"Thank goodness," says Rosa.

Philippe continues to howl.

"I have an idea," says Uncle Louis. "I think I know of a

way to stop his crying. But I don't think *you* will want to do it, Rosa. Sander has told me some terrible things about you."

"Terrible things?"

"Yes. He's told me that you never want to touch your violin again." Uncle Louis strokes his chin. "You see, if you were to play your violin a little bit for Philippe, I'm sure that he would be quiet. But *you* don't want to play anymore. You don't want to become Rosa Rosevici, do you? Oh, well, we artists can't be forced. It's such a shame, such a shame. Philippe is so…"

"All right, I'll play. I'll do it for Philippe."

"Are you sure? Of course, it's partly your fault that he's crying, isn't it?"

Rosa nods. "Yes," she replies. "It's because of that cold wet washcloth."

"Cold wet washcloth? What do you mean?"

"Nothing. I'll get my violin."

Rosa crawls under her bed. The violin has been lying in its case underneath the bed for a long time now. She opens the case, picks up her violin, and begins to play:

Sleep, baby, sleep,
Outside there roams a sheep…

Uncle Louis rocks his son in his arms. Philippe has stopped crying. He looks at his father with wide-open eyes. Slowly his eyes begin to close.

"He's sleeping," Uncle Louis whispers. "I'll put him back into his crib." He rises, and carefully tucks Philippe in. "Have a good night. See you in the morning, sweetheart."

"You won't be letting Philippe sleep in our room anymore, will you?" asks Rosa fearfully.

"Did you let him fall on purpose?"

"Of course not," answers Silvie, and she glares at him.

"Well, then. But if he ever cries so long and so hard again…ahem…we heard him the entire evening, I'm afraid…then…"

"If he ever cries so long and so hard again, I'll play the violin for him," Rosa promises.

"Good." Uncle Louis winks at Silvie. "But then you'd better make sure that you know more songs than just 'Sleep, Baby, Sleep.'"

"I'll practice a lot. I'll practice all the children's songs I know."

He winks at Silvie again. "As long as you don't practice *too* hard. We wouldn't be able to stand all that racket. And now: sleep, children, sleep."

He tiptoes to the door. The girls can hear him walking down the steps.

"Good night, Silvie."

"Good night, Rosa."

All kinds of little sounds are coming from the crib.

"Oh, no. Don't wake up, Philippe," Rosa begs. "Please don't. I'm tired, and my violin is tired, too."

"Ta, ta. Papapam."

"Don't answer him," Silvie whispers, and she puts her head under her pillow.

Not a sound is coming from the little bed now. Not a sound is coming from the big beds, either.

◆ Mrs. Levie

"Something terrible is going to happen to Mrs. Levie next week," says Silvie, and she takes a bite of her gelatin pudding. "Something very, very terrible."

"What are you talking about?" Mama is so startled that she forgets to bring her spoon to her mouth. "How did you learn about this?"

"I heard it myself," Silvie answers, and she continues eating.

"Put your spoon down. I want to know what you mean." Mama grasps Silvie's hand. "Tell me."

"Mrs. Levie is going to die next week."

"*Die?*"

"Yes, die. That's what she said to Mr. Rozeboom."

"What exactly did she say?"

"Mr. Rozeboom asked when she was going to give her life to the new citizen of the world, and Mrs. Levie said, 'Next week.'"

"Oh, Silvie!" Mama exclaims, and she bursts out laughing. She is shaking so hard that her pudding is quivering on her spoon.

"You shouldn't laugh when someone is going to die," says Silvie. "That's mean."

"I think so, too," Rosa adds.

"Listen to me for a minute." Mama takes her napkin and wipes the tears from her eyes. "Giving life to a world citizen has nothing to do with dying. It means that a baby is going to be born. The mother gives the child *its* life, not her own life. The mother—Mrs. Levie,

83

that is—will remain alive. She's not giving her own life away."

"Oh," whispers Silvie. "Thank goodness."

"Wait." Mama stands up. "I have something to show you." She walks to the living room. "Where did I put all those things?" they hear her mutter. "Ha, there it is."

Mama sits down at the table again. "Let me take a look...yes, this is yours," she says, and she lays a newspaper clipping on Rosa's plate. "And this is yours," she continues, and she lays a clipping on Silvie's plate, too.

"Read the announcement out loud. Read yours first, Rosa."

Rosa begins:

> *On Sunday, December 13, 1931,*
> *Mrs. M. de Jong-de Roos*
> *gave life to a well-made daughter*
> *Rosa*
> *Mother and child are in good condition.*
>
> H. de Jong.
> M. de Jong-de Roos.

"That's me," says Rosa, and she giggles. "A well-made daughter. How funny. What does 'well-made' mean?"

"It means that you were all there," Mama explains. "Everything was complete, hands, feet, everything. Now your turn, Silvie. What does your birth announcement say?"

Silvie reads:

> *On Wednesday March 28, 1935*
> *Mrs. M. de Jong-de Roos*

gave life to a well-made daughter
Silvie
Sister of Rosa.
Mother and child are in good condition.
Please do not disturb between the hours of
one and four o'clock.

H. de Jong.
M. de Jong-de Roos.
Rosa.

"You read that very well, Silvie. You're a clever girl," says their mother. "Your birth announcement is longer than Rosa's. Now take a good look at me." She stands up on her chair. "Am I dead?"

Rosa and Silvie look up at her face.

"You're alive," says Silvie.

"Definitely alive," adds Rosa.

"Well then. I don't want you to have any more of those gloomy thoughts. Maybe we can buy a gift for the new citizen of the world." Mama jumps off her chair.

"Mrs. Levie has hardly any baby clothes," says Rosa. "She gave away Loetje's old clothes to a woman who went to Westerbork with her baby."

"How do you know?" asks Mama.

"That's what Mrs. Levie told Mr. Rozeboom when we were doing our arithmetic. I heard it, too," says Silvie.

"Miss Know-It-All," Mama says to her. "*You* know everything, as well. But now I have an idea. I've saved all your baby clothes, and I don't think that we'll have another baby. Let's go up to the attic on Sunday, and gather all our baby clothes together. On Monday you can bring them to school in paper bags, and give them to Mrs. Levie, for her new baby. All right?"

"Yes!" says Rosa.

"That's a wonderful idea," Silvie exclaims.

Mama and the girls are sitting on the attic floor. There are baby clothes everywhere. Pants, diapers, navel bands, socks, sweaters...

"How adorable!" Mama calls. "Silvie got that vest from Grandma de Roos. She knit it herself. And oh...look at this, what a darling sunbonnet. And..." She picks up a handful of clothes. "They're so sweet, aren't they?" she whispers. She pats a sleeper, and sniffs it. "It smells like Palmolive Soap. It *should* smell like that, too, because when you were little I washed you with Palmolive. Sander used to draw advertisements for the factory that made the soap, and every week he would bring me a couple of bars. Everything still smells like soap, because when I stored away the clothes, I put the empty soap wrappers between them."

"When we were at Sander's house on his birthday, we say those ads in his studio," says Silvie. "There were five little girls in the picture. They were quintuplets from Canada, I think."

"Come on. We'll never finish at the rate we're going," says Rosa impatiently. "When Mrs. Levie gives life to a well-made baby next week, we'll still be sitting here in the attic."

"Shall I walk with you and help carry something?" Mama reaches for the bag that Silvie is holding. It is from Het Kleine Paradijs.

"Rosa, remember when Papa and I took you to Het Kleine Paradijs to buy clothes, and you picked out a yellow woolen dress?" asks Mama. "You just *had* to have it. You wouldn't settle for anything else, even though it was the height of summer."

"The star doesn't show up very well on yellow," Rosa explains. "That's why I wanted the dress, and I didn't care that I was practically suffocating from the heat when I wore it. You don't have to help us, Mama. Come on, Silvie, let's go."

Silvie raises the bag of clothes high above her head. "See how strong I am!" she calls.

Rosa has her school bag in one hand. In her other hand she is holding two large bags full of clothes. She will have to carry them very carefully. Imagine what would happen if the bags tore and all the diapers and socks and sweaters fell onto the street! "Those Jewish children are always doing strange things. Ordinary children don't take baby clothes to school," people would say.

It is late. They are walking slower than usual.

"We've got to hurry," says Rosa. "It's already ten minutes after nine."

They run to the Juliana van Stolbergstraat. "Look," Silvie pants. "There is a line of people in front of number twenty-nine. It's our class. They're all standing outside."

The girls slow down, and stop at the gate of number twenty-nine.

"We can't go to school," says Ruth. "Mrs. Levie won't open the door, and Mr. Levie won't, either."

"Hello!" A woman is leaning out of the window next door.

"Hello!" she calls again. "They're gone, the poor things.

Yes, they were taken from their home last night. The noise woke me up, and I couldn't go back to sleep. Yes, little Loetje is gone, too. He looked so sweet when he left, with a teddy bear under his arm. Well, you'll be all right, won't you? I'm going to try to go back to sleep."

The window closes with a bang.

"We'll have to go home now," says Mr. Rozeboom. "Go home. I don't know what else to do anymore."

Together they walk toward the beginning of the street. When the children reach the first house, they go their separate ways.

"Goodbye, see you later."

"Yes, see you later."

Rosa and Silvie head toward home, dragging their feet as they go. They don't say a word.

A pink sock falls to the sidewalk. Silvie starts to pick it up.

"Don't. Just leave it," says Rosa.

◆ *Snow in June*

Rosa doesn't want to think about Mr. and Mrs. Levie and Loetje today. She wants to dream about pleasant things. She curls up in the big chair, which is beginning to creak a little. It sounds as though it is saying something to her. When Rosa moves, the chair speaks. When she sits quietly, the chair is quiet, too.

Rosa shuts her eyes, but not too tightly. Perhaps she will have nicer dreams then.

She is standing near her old school in the Beetslaan. She takes a few steps on the playground. She peers through a window, and sees her own class. The teacher, Mr. Van der Lans, is talking to his students. Rosa hardly dares look to see who is sitting at her desk. When she finally does manage to look, she sees a child who must be new to the class. It is a girl with blond braids that are wrapped in a coil around her ears.

"Get out of my seat!" Rosa shouts. "That's *my* place!"

The child doesn't move. Rosa takes a step closer. She is standing right by the window now. Is Mr. Van der Lans looking at her? Yes. "Come in!" he is saying, and he gestures to her.

"I'm not allowed to!" She points to the star on her chest.

The teacher opens the window. "Come in," he says. "I'll help you. We'll just take the star off." He reaches for a pair of large scissors, and begins to remove the star from her dress. "The sewing teacher will mend that hole in your dress," he says. "I cut it by accident."

"That doesn't matter," says Rosa.

"Go to your seat." Mr. Van der Lans takes her by the hand.

"I can't. Someone is sitting there."

"Then I know what to do." He points to the new child. "Ilse, you take the desk in the back." He gathers the blond girl's books and papers, and places them on the desk at the back of the room.

"I'm going to tell my father on you," Ilse whines. "He will punish you for putting a German child in the last row."

"Go right ahead and tell him," says Mr. Van der Lans, and he turns to the class. "Children, it's time to sing our welcoming song for Rosa. One, two, three." He waves his arms. The class begins to sing:

Rosa, Rosa, we think it's so fine
That you're now in our class,
We think it's divine!
We'll help you with reading,
We'll help you with math,
We'll help you with language,
Just follow our path.

All the children are singing except Ilse, who is biting into an apple.

"Rosa may now stand on my chair," says the teacher. "Come on."

Rosa climbs up on his chair.

"We'll sing the song one more time," he says.

"Rosa, Rosa..."

The door opens, and the school principal enters the room.

"Rosa is back," Mr. Van der Lans tells him.

"I can't keep track of all the students who get sick," says the principal. "I'm glad that you're feeling better now."

Rosa doesn't answer. The principal disappears.

"Take your seat," says Mr. Van der Lans. "We'll sing for you later."

Rosa sits down at her old desk. The books that the children are reading are full of numbers. Rosa looks at Martha's book. The numbers are beginning to move. They are flying out of the book, and settling on her head, on her shoulders, in her eyes.

"I've got to get out of here!" she shouts.

"No, you've just come. I'm not opening the window," says the teacher, and he grins.

Rosa runs to the window. It's locked. She runs to the door. It is locked, too.

Or is it? The door opens, and a man enters the room. He is wearing a policeman's hat and black boots. "Are there any Jewish children here?" he asks. "I smell Jewish children!"

Rosa remains frozen before the class. She is going to be taken away now.

What is this? All the children in her class have stood up from their seats. They are forming a circle around her. She can no longer see the policeman. The children are carrying flowers, armloads of flowers, and they are all for Rosa. Flowers are everywhere: on her head, on her back, in the hole in her dress. She is being buried in flowers!

"There must be a party taking place in here," says the policeman. "I'm leaving. I don't see any Jewish children." He strides out of the room.

The children are still standing in a circle around Rosa.

"Thank you," she whispers.

"You don't have to thank us," says Mr. Van der Lans. "Do you think that it would ever occur to us to betray a classmate? No, we're not like that at the Beetslaan School. You may take all the flowers home with you. And if I were you,

I would go home now, in case that policeman comes back again."

Rosa floats to the window. The window opens by itself. With her arms full of flowers, she floats outside and up into the sky. She is very happy.

German soldiers are walking in the street down below. Rosa can hear them singing. Should she startle them a bit? Should she drop a flower on them? She tears the petals from a white flower, and scatters them beneath her.

"Snow!" she hears someone shout. "*Es schneit*. In the middle of the summer!"

Rosa begins to laugh. How wonderful it is to drift through the sky with an armful of flowers and make it snow! She tears the petals from all the flowers, and lets them fall down below. No one will understand what is happening. The soldiers are looking up at the sky, but they can't see where the snow is coming from.

Rosa can't stop laughing. She coughs.

"It's happening again," she hears her father say. "She's having another attack. I'll fetch a doctor now. We've got to get a doctor. The child isn't well. You're not well, are you, Rosa?"

Mama lays her hand against Rosa's forehead. "The only thing she needs is some diversion," she says. "Right, Rosa?"

Rosa doesn't answer. She is dreaming.

◆ Prince Vladimir

"One, two, three, four, five, six, seven, eight." Silvie counts the chiming of the clock. "It's eight o'clock. We can't go outside now. And it's such nice weather."

She walks to the window. "Marja is playing out there," she says. "And Kees de Bruin is walking his dog." She spits against the window. "Rotten Marja, rotten Kees!" she calls.

"Come sit next to me on the sofa," says Mama. "I'll tell you another story about Sander."

"Whenever something bad happens, *you* start telling stories," says Rosa, glaring at her. "When Mr. Nuszbaum was taken away, you did it, too. I'm not a little child anymore."

"Don't you want to hear about Sander and Prince Vladimir?"

"Prince Vladimir?"

"Yes."

"All right, tell us."

The girls cuddle next to their mother. Mama puts an arm around each of them, and begins her story.

"Sander was almost four years old when he started nursery school. He didn't want me to walk with him, because the school was close to our house. He came home around noon that first day. He ran into the kitchen, and called, 'We have a prince at school. From Russia!'

"'A prince? How do you know that he's a prince?' asked Grandma.

"'I can tell he's a prince. He looks so grand. He has on velvet pants and a golden crown.'

"'A crown?'

"'Yes, a golden crown, and because he's so grand, all the children in the class had to sing a song for him. I had to sing, too.'

"'What did you sing?'

"'May He Live a Long Life. He's royalty, just like Puss in Boots.'

"I hardly dared to look at Grandma, because I was trying not to laugh, but Sander remained dead serious.

"'Have a sandwich. It's almost time for you to go back to school,' said Grandma.

"Sander didn't move. 'What does a prince eat for lunch?' he asked.

"'What do you think, Sander? Maybe a peanut butter sandwich, just like you.'

"'Oh, no he doesn't. He eats rolls with golden sprinkles. And he has chocolate milk with whipped cream, and he drinks it through a straw.' Sander ate his peanut butter sandwich and returned to school.

"When he came home that afternoon, he sat down on the sofa. 'We had to sing for the Russian prince again, and I don't want to sing for him tomorrow.'

"'What is the prince's name?' I asked.

"'Vladimir.'

"'Nice name. And what did you have to sing?'

"'Long Shall He Live. And then we had to eat cookies. And he had to give cookies to the children in the other classes. Oh, he's very, very rich. I can tell.'"

Rosa and Silvie are rolling over with laughter.

"He thought that a little boy who was celebrating his birthday was a Russian prince!" Silvie shrieks. "And he had to eat cookies. With a crown on his head."

"Crazy Sander," says Rosa, laughing. She walks toward the window, but stops in the middle of the room. "Oh no, we're having a thunderstorm. And it's pouring down rain."

"It's been storming all this time, but luckily you didn't notice," says their mother. "Did I ever tell you about the time when Sander painted his scooter with dog poop?"

"No more stories," says Rosa. "I want to read now."

Silvie walks to the window. She wipes it clean with her petticoat.

"Now Marja and Kees have to stay in, too," she says. "It serves them right."

◆ A Normal Day

"I want so much to have a *normal* day," says Silvie. "A day like I used to have when I was still five."

"We'll do it," says Lita Rosa, and she pulls Silvie onto her lap. "We'll spend a normal Wednesday afternoon together. Just as we used to do, before the war. For that's what you mean, isn't it? Will you join us, Rosa?"

"Oh, yes." Rosa sits on her aunt's lap, too. "What will we be doing?"

"Don't you remember?" Lita Rosa looks at Rosa in surprise. "We'll make pancakes, of course. How could you forget that? Ask your mother if it's all right with her."

Silvie runs into the kitchen. She returns a moment later.

"She says it's all right. She thinks it's a nice idea, but we have to be home before eight o'clock."

"That goes without saying," says Lita Rosa.

The day has come. The girls are on their way to Lita Rosa's and Uncle Jossie's house.

Rosa and Silvie have been looking forward to the normal afternoon. Lita Rosa has promised that they will act as if the war did not exist. They will not be talking about people who have been taken away, even though those people may well be in their thoughts.

Together they baked a cake for their aunt and uncle, a very pretty one with bits of fruit on top. They wrapped it in gold paper, which Mama had saved from prewar days. Silvie is carrying it.

"You lead the way to Lita Rosa's," she says, "and I'll take care of the cake."

The girls almost pass by the house. Suddenly, they are standing right in front. Before they have a chance to ring the doorbell, the door flies open. Lita Rosa is standing in the doorway.

"Hello, my dears. Come in. Let's celebrate a normal day now," she says, and she wraps her arms around them. How nice and soft she is!

Rosa gives her sister a little push. "Hand it over," she says.

Silvie doesn't move. She stares at her aunt.

"What's the matter?" asks Lita Rosa, and she laughs. "I look pretty, don't I? Do you like my hair bow? I just bought it."

"It's nice," says Silvie. "Here is a cake for you. Rosa and I made it ourselves."

"Mmm, wonderful." Lita Rosa smacks her lips. "We'll unwrap it when Jossie get home. He'll be here soon. And now...come inside."

Silvie dashes into the living room. "Oh!" she calls. She runs to the dining room table. "Cookies and punch and tea. Where shall I sit?"

"At your own place, next to me. I'll lift you up." Lita Rosa puts Silvie in a chair. "And Rosa, you sit over there, next to Jossie's place." She points to the other side of the table. "I'm going into the kitchen. I have a surprise for you there."

Lita Rosa returns a few moments later. "Here I am again. What do you think is inside?" she asks, and she lays two little packages on the table. "Oh, well, you wouldn't be able to guess, anyway. Open them. I'll count to three. One, two, three!"

Rosa is the first to unwrap her package. "Mmm, delicious!" she cries.

"Oh, a nougat bar, just like the ones we used to eat!" Silvie shouts. She bites into it. "You eat yours, too," she says to Rosa.

"What a good time we're having, aren't we?" says Lita Rosa, and she laughs. "Tea and cookies and two sweet nieces. What more could a person want? What do you want to do now? Shall we put on a play? No? Well, then we won't. I'll pour you something to drink first."

The girls drink their punch in small sips, to make it last longer. Their hands are sticky, and their faces are dirty from the chocolate, which covered the nougat like a jacket.

"This is fun, isn't it?" says Lita Rosa. "Are you enjoying the afternoon, too? It's just the way it used to be when you were five, Silvie."

"Not completely," says Rosa softly. "When she was five, we didn't have to wear a star."

"We'll do something about that right away." Lita Rosa stands up. "Our stars are sewn onto our vests, aren't they? We'll just take the vests off then, and hang them on the coat rack in the hall. Hup, we'll be normal again. Off with those stars! I don't know who it was who came up with the idea of sewing these rotten stars on a vest like this. Do you remember that when we first started wearing a star, we sewed one on every single dress and blouse? It's much easier this way. Long live the inventor of the vest with the star, which we can simply put on over our clothes.

"That's not fair." Silvie is almost in tears. "We were supposed to have a normal day today."

"You're right," says Lita Rosa. "We won't hang them up in the hall, for the whole world to see. We'll hide them under a sofa cushion. All right?"

"We're not allowed to be without a star," says Rosa. "If you don't wear a star, you could be taken away."

"We don't have to wear a star in the house," says Lita Rosa. She takes their vests to the sofa and stuffs them under the cushions. "Go away, you stinky things," she says. "There, now we're normal again. An aunt and two nieces who are going to celebrate a normal day."

"I want to play *sjoelbak*," says Rosa.

"Fine, I'll go get the game." Lita Rosa has already left the room.

"I'm going to win," Silvie exclaims.

They play *sjoelbak*, just as they used to do. They play so hard that every now and then the pieces fly over the edge of the board. The harder the girls play, the hotter they become.

"Look who's here." Lita Rosa forgets to throw her piece.

"Uncle Jossie!" Rosa and Silvie run to the hall.

"I'll open the door. Come on, we'll go meet him!" Rosa calls.

They run outside. "Come in, Uncle Jossie! You've got to make pancakes for us!"

Uncle Jossie does not look happy at all. What could the matter be? "Take my briefcase," he says to Rosa. "Hurry!"

He puts an arm around each girl, and covers their chests with his hands. "Walk quickly," he whispers. "You're not wearing a star. Go on, keep walking."

Rosa is too frightened to move. Uncle Jossie pulls her by her dress. "Hurry up, sweetheart," he says.

They walk to the house. Lita Rosa is standing in the doorway.

"Hello, Jossie, we... What's wrong with you? You're as white as a sheet," she exclaims.

"They weren't wearing a star. My God, darling, *you* aren't wearing one, either."

"They couldn't help it. It was my fault." Lita Rosa puts her hands over her face, and begins to cry.

"Let's go inside," says Uncle Jossie. "Don't cry, sweetheart."

His arms are still wrapped around Rosa and Silvie. He wipes his feet on the doormat, then closes the door with his foot.

The girls are sitting at the table, wearing their vests once again. They are eating wonderful, sweet pancakes. Their cheeks are sticky from the syrup, and grains of sugar are trapped between their fingers.

"Is it good?" Uncle Jossie asks.

"It's delicious," says Lita Rosa.

"What did you do while I was away?" he asks.

"We played *sjoelbak*," Silvie answers. "And we had a normal afternoon."

Uncle Jossie glances at his watch. "It's seven-thirty. You've got to go. I'll take you home."

Rosa looks at her watch, as well. "It's much too early to leave," she protests. "It only takes fifteen minutes to walk home. And I haven't finished my pancake yet."

"But I have to walk back home, too," Uncle Jossie sighs. "I'll wrap up the rest of your pancake, and you can take it with you," he says.

"You'd better get going," says Lita Rosa. "You know what can happen if we're out on the street after eight o'clock. We could be…"

Silvie puts her hand over Lita Rosa's mouth. "Don't," she whispers. "Let's be normal for just a *little* bit longer."

◆ *Buying Cauliflower*

"Oh, dear," says Mama, and she stamps her foot on the kitchen floor. "Now that I'm ready to cook supper for this evening, I see that we're out of vegetables. We've got to buy some cauliflower. Will you go shopping for me, Rosa? I'm so busy at the moment. Lita Rosa and Jossie will be eating with us tonight. If you had gone to their house a little later yesterday, you could have shopped for me then. Go now, Rosa, to make up for it."

"Right now?"

"Yes, what did you think? I need the cauliflower now."

"Silly Mama."

"Silly? Why am I silly?"

"You should know."

"No, I don't know. Now hurry up." Mama wipes her hands on her flowered apron. "Here is my purse. Get going."

"What time is it, Mama?"

"Quarter to twelve."

"That's why I can't buy cauliflower now. The only time Jews may go shopping is between three and five o'clock in the afternoon," says Rosa, trying to look like a German soldier as she speaks.

"Oh, that's right." Mama collapses into a chair. She buries her face in her hands. "I forgot about that," she says with a sob. "And I'm so tired, so sick and tired of everything."

"Don't worry. I'll go as soon as it's three o'clock," Rosa promises, and she strokes her mother's hair. "Don't cry."

Mama puts her hands down. Her eyes are very red. "I'm all right now." She sobs a little, and tries to laugh at the same time. "What's wrong with me? What do *you* think, Rosa?"

"You're tired. Didn't you just say so yourself?"

"You're sweet. You're a sweet girl," says Mama. "Come here. I want to give you a great big kiss. And you don't need to take the shopping bag when you go out to buy that one cauliflower."

RETA E. KING LIBRARY
CHADRON STATE COLLEGE
CHADRON, NE 69337

Standing outside the grocery store, Rosa looks at the clock that hangs on the wall of the store. She isn't wearing her watch because it is broken, but she can look through the window and see the clock very easily.

It's ten minutes before three. She'll have to wait ten more minutes. She steps aside, to allow the other customers to walk past.

Five minutes to three. How slowly the time is passing! She jumps from one leg to the other. In a little while the store will be sold out of everything. That happened to her once, when she wanted to buy some lettuce. Only one customer is inside, a woman who is wearing a striped dress.

Finally it is three o'clock, and Rosa may go in now. She wipes her feet, and looks at the clock once again. Three o'clock.

"Well? What can I do for you?" asks the grocer from behind the counter. Is he looking at Rosa? Is it really her turn? The woman in the striped dress has completed her shopping and is busily packing her grocery bag.

"What would you like? Yes, you," the grocer says to Rosa.

"I want a large cauliflower."

"Stop!"

Rosa is pushed to the side. "I'm first. It's not three o'clock yet." A tall boy is holding his wristwatch under her nose. He taps his finger against the crystal. "Five minutes to three. That clock is fast," he says rudely, and points to the clock on the wall. "Five minutes to three. If I see you coming in early again, I'll report you to the Germans. Then you and your family will be..."

Rosa doesn't wait for him to finish. She runs outside, and stands in front of the store. Her legs are shaking so badly that she can't go any further. She watches the boy as he leaves the store, carrying a large shopping bag. Perhaps there is a cauliflower inside. She turns away. She doesn't want him to see her, for she is afraid that he will start lecturing her about the clock again.

"Wait a minute, Gustaaf." The woman in the striped dress is walking behind the boy. She pulls him by his belt. "Stop right there." He turns around.

"If you *ever* behave like that again, I'm going to tell your parents. I've lived next door to your family long enough to know that your father and mother don't share your beliefs, you ugly brat. You're a dirty little traitor, that's what you are. What's in your bag? Lettuce and cauliflower? I thought so. Hand it over. Then she'll have two. I bought a cauliflower for her as well."

The boy gives his bag to the woman. She reaches in, and takes out a large cauliflower. "That's a nice one," she says to Rosa. "Here, take it. One from him, and one from me."

The boy slinks away. His shopping bag is dangling from his shoulder.

"Thank you," Rosa whispers.

"You don't have to thank me," the woman answers. "I'll continue to oppose those Nazis, even if the war lasts a hundred years."

"Oh, no," says Rosa. "Not a hundred years!"

"Of course not. Silly girl. Shall I tell you something? The occupation will last for six more months at the most, and then they'll leave, the filthy swine. And we'll be free. We'll be free then, do you hear me? Before June nineteen forty-three!"

"Shhh, not so loud," says Rosa, and she looks around, afraid that someone will hear what this nice woman is saying. Talking out loud in such a manner is dangerous.

"You're right." The woman speaks quietly now. "Sometimes I'm not very careful. Goodbye. Go right home, and I hope you enjoy the cauliflower." Picking up her shopping bag, which she had set down on the sidewalk, she walks away.

"*Two* cauliflowers?" says Mama, when Rosa is home again.

"Yes, and here is all your money back." She lets the money fall into her mother's hand. "I got everything for nothing."

"How can that be? You didn't steal them, did you?"

"Of course not. I came by them in an honest way. Someone gave them to me, and it was all because I went into the store before three o'clock. I didn't have my watch on, and the store clock was fast."

"You went in before three? Oh, no." Mama looks at Rosa. "How dangerous. You know we could all be taken away because of that. And I've certainly changed. Years ago, I never would have approved of your getting food that way. The next time you go shopping for me, you'll have to be more careful about the time."

"I'm never going shopping again," says Rosa. "Never, ever again."

◆ Dog

Rosa and Silvie are sitting with three friends on the fence outside the music school, across from the park. All the children live on the Broekslootkade: Rina and Ruben live at Number Seventy-nine, and Mirjam lives at Number Eighty-three. They are talking about their parents, grandparents, aunts, and uncles.

"All of our grandpas and grandmas have been taken away," says Silvie.

"They say that my grandparents are hiding. It's called 'being in hiding,'" Ruben whispers. "But I don't believe it."

"What is it called?" Mirjam leans over toward him. "Say it louder."

Ruben tries to look mysterious. "I can't," he whispers. "I'm not really supposed to talk about it. It's a secret. If the Nazis hear me, they'll take me away and torture me until I tell where they are."

"Do you know where your grandparents are?" asks Rosa. She is whispering, too.

"They're...they're..." Ruben's voice is barely audible. "Someone brought them to the South of France, to Avignon. They had to take a train through Belgium and France. And the Germans let them do it."

"That's impossible," exclaims Mirjam, jumping off the fence. She stands across from him. "You're lying," she says. "What a liar you are, Ruben. There are Germans in France, too."

"Not everywhere. They're not in the South of France. And I'm not telling you anything more now." Ruben presses his lips together.

"It's a good thing, too." Rina jumps off the fence as well. "If you say anything else, I'm going to tell Papa and Mama. You know you're not supposed to talk about it. What you're doing is very dangerous."

"Dirty tattletale. My sister is a dirty tattletale!"

"I am not!"

"You are, too! Tattletale, tattletale, you shouldn't...ouch!" Rina and Ruben are rolling on the ground.

"Look out!" Mirjam shouts. "There's a dog coming by, and its creepy owner, too." She tries to pull Ruben and Rina apart, but she can't. They continue to fight.

"Come!" a woman calls to her dog. "Come here, Chang. Just let those Jewish children keep fighting. Don't bother with them. Let them tear each other apart. Come, I say!"

The little dog walks back to its owner, who is standing a bit farther down the sidewalk.

Rina and Ruben have stopped fighting. They are sitting next to each other on the fence once again.

"I'm glad that rotten little Pekinese didn't bother you," says Rosa, laughing. "It might have bitten you. Look, it's going into the park with that horrible woman."

"That dog is a little Nazi," says Mirjam. "I've seen its owner wearing an N.S.B. pin on her coat. She belongs to the Nazi Party. I know that for sure."

"Are you positive?" Ruben is beginning to whisper again. "Let's see if she has the pin on right now. Too bad we're not allowed in the park. And that bratty dog *is* allowed to go there! Let's wait by the fence. If the woman really is wearing an N.S.B. pin, we'll do something to her dog. Throw rocks at it, maybe."

"If she sees us doing that, we'll go to prison," says Rina. "Besides, it's not the dog's fault that it has such a terrible owner."

"You're such a good little girl," Ruben sneers, and he sticks his tongue out at his sister. "Papa and Mama will think you're such a good little girl."

"Can't we do something to the dog without actually hurting it?" asks Rosa.

"Ohhh, Rosa is a good little girl, too. Just like my sister."

Rosa doesn't answer. She is a little bit afraid of Ruben. Thank goodness she doesn't have a brother like him!

"That dog is sometimes out alone in the morning. We could do something to it then, and that creepy woman would never know," Mirjam whispers.

"Run to the park. There they are!" Ruben calls, and he jumps off the fence. The girls run with him. They stop at the entrance, directly under the sign that says FORBIDDEN FOR JEWS. They see that the dog is not moving.

"I hope it poops all over the entire park," Ruben whispers. "I want there to be mountains and mountains of poop, so that everyone slips on the piles."

"That rotten dog is raising up its leg. It's going to pee against the tree," says Rosa, and she giggles. "You should see what a stream it's making."

"I've got it!" Ruben exclaims. "Now I know what we can do. Rosa, when you said 'That rotten dog is raising up its leg,' you gave me an idea. If that woman is an N.S.B.-er, I'll make a cardboard sign tonight, and tie it around the dog's neck tomorrow. And do you know what I'll put on the sign? I RAISE MY PAW AND SALUTE HITLER, TOO."

"I raise my paw and salute Hitler, too? I think you're a little bit crazy," says Rina, pointing to her forehead. "You're crazy, Ruben."

"Let me explain," he says. "Has anyone seen how two Germans greet each other?"

"I have!" says Mirjam.

"What do they do?" Rina asks.

"They raise their right arms up at a slant, and call 'Heil Hitler,'" Ruben answers. "In other words—"

"Stop, Ruben. I understand!" Rosa exclaims, and laughs so hard that Ruben puts his hand over her mouth.

"Quiet." He begins to laugh, too. "In other words, when Nazis greet each other, they raise up their arms. So if we're sure that she's an N.S.B.-er, I'll write on the sign...oh, oh, here comes the dog again."

The little dog walks to the exit of the park. The woman approaches as well.

"Here, Chang!" she calls. The dog trots back to her.

"Look...look at her collar," Rosa stammers. "She's wearing an N.S.B. pin."

"Come to my house at nine o'clock tomorrow morning. We're really going to go through with this. And don't say anything about it to your parents," Ruben warns them.

At the stroke of nine, Rosa and Mirjam appear in front of the door of Number Seventy-nine. Rosa must stand on tiptoe to reach the copper bell.

"Let me ring it," says Mirjam. "I'm taller than you." She pulls on the doorbell. No one answers. She rings again.

The door to Number Eighty-one opens.

"Hello, Mrs. Boerstra," says Mirjam. "Do you know where—"

Mrs. Boerstra puts her finger to her lips. "Shhh," she says. "I have something to give to you. Last night Ruben came over with a blue package. 'Don't ask me anything about it,' he said. 'But will you please give this package to Rosa and Mirjam? Just tell them it's a little gift for Chang.'"

The woman looks at Rosa. "Are there Chinese people in your family?" she inquires.

"No."

"Oh, and do you know what else Ruben said? 'Mrs. Boerstra,' he said, 'I don't want to bring it to Rosa's or Mirjam's house, because that would be too dangerous. They could be taken away tonight.'"

"Ruben wasn't taken away," says Mirjam. "If the Germans had come for him, there would have been a lot of noise, just as there was when the Kooperbergs at Number Eighty-seven were taken away."

"I think you're right," says Mrs. Boerstra. "I think that they went into hiding."

"Or maybe they fled to Avignon," Rosa whispers in Mirjam's ear.

Mrs. Boerstra closes her door a little. "You've got to go now," she says. "It's a shame that you're not allowed to come inside. Here is the present for Chang."

Rosa takes the package.

"Shall we go to my house?" asks Mirjam.

"All right. Let me tell my mother first."

"What are you going to tell her?"

"That I'm going to your house."

"Oh, I thought you were going to tell her about the package," says Mirjam, relieved.

"Of course not. What are we going to do with it now?" Rosa asks.

"I'm afraid to put that sign on the dog," says Mirjam.

"I am, too."

"Tonight when it's dark, we'll throw it into the canal in front of your house," says Mirjam. "Give it to me. I'll do it." She reaches for the sign. "Give it here."

"We can't do it tonight. It stays light much too long. We have to be inside by eight o'clock." Rosa is nearly in tears. "Should we take the package back to Mrs. Boerstra?"

"No," says Mirjam. "Come with me. We'll throw it in the water now. You look to make sure that no one is coming, and I'll throw it in."

They walk to the canal. Rosa stands with her back to the water.

"One, two, three," Mirjam counts. Rosa can hear the sound of water splashing.

"Run!" Mirjam shouts. "It's still floating!"

They hurry toward Mirjam's house. "I won't tell my mother where I am right now," Rosa pants. "I'm too afraid."

Mirjam can barely open the front door. When the girls are finally inside, they rush up to the attic. Trembling, they huddle next to each other. They don't want to come downstairs until they have calmed down a bit.

"I'd better go," says Rosa, after half an hour. My mother will be worried about me."

They walk down the steps together.

"Rosa, I didn't know that you were here," says Mirjam's mother, when she sees them.

"Yes," says Rosa, "but I'm leaving now."

When Rosa is standing in front of her house, she turns to look at the water once again.

The package has disappeared. There are only ducks floating in the canal now.

◆ Friend

It is Sunday afternoon. Rosa and Silvie are playing checkers.
Uncle Louis is painting. Papa, Mama, and Aunt Isabelle
are reading. Philippe is sleeping at last.

"I have to stop in a little while," says Rosa.

"Don't. I'll be bored if you do." Silvie begins to build a
tower with the pieces she has won from her sister.

"I have to," says Rosa, and she slaps the checkerboard
so hard that the pieces fly up into the air. "When I was
playing Philippe to sleep a few minutes ago, I saw how dull
my violin looked. I'm going to polish it until it's so shiny
that I can see my face in it. I've already put it under my
chair."

"I want you to keep playing checkers with me," Silvie
grumbles.

Mama lays her book in her lap. "What did we use to do
on Sundays?" she asks. "Do you know that I can hardly
remember anymore?"

"That's strange." Father puts his book down, too. "Don't
you remember that we would often take a ride in the car?
And that we would also take Rosa and Silvie to the
playground?"

"And we'd get a nougat bar wrapped in silver paper, just
like the one we had when we went to Lita Rosa's house,"
Rosa exclaims. "And we'd go on the swings, and there was
a fortuneteller at the playground, too, and..."

"That was before the war," says Mama, and she sighs.
"What I mean is, what did we do at the beginning of the
war? How did we spend our Sundays then?"

Papa begins to pace the living room floor. "We used to visit Jan and Mieke, and Kees and Joke. We rode our bicycles, remember?"

Mama nods unhappily. "We can't do that anymore," she says. "They've taken all our non-Jewish friends away from us."

Silvie stands on her chair. "I know what you mean," she says. "Let me announce it: Ladies and gentlemen, Jews may no longer have telephones, and Jews may no longer visit non-Jews!"

She jumps off the chair. "And we can't ride bicycles anymore, either, because the Nazis have swiped them. And how do I know, ladies and gentlemen? I know because it was in the newspaper, and it was on our list, and Sander has written things on our list, too, in red ink."

"We'd often listen to the radio on Sunday afternoon," Uncle Louis remarks.

"We no longer have a radio, either!" Silvie calls, and she stands on her chair again. "May first, nineteen forty-one. Jews must turn in their radios."

"Stop it! Sit down in your chair and finish your game," says Father. He grabs Silvie by the arm, and pulls her down onto the seat. "I don't find it one bit amusing when you rattle off all those prohibitions. Hearing them one after another like that just makes it seem worse."

"It's bad enough even when you don't rattle them off," says Rosa. "Don't be angry with me, Papa, but you often do it yourself. And listening to you talk about all these terrible things gives me a stomachache."

The doorbell! Uncle Louis lays his brush on a saucer. Rosa and Silvie stop playing checkers. Papa and Mama put their books down.

"There is someone at the door," Aunt Isabelle whispers. "Who could it be? The Rosenberg family was taken away yesterday afternoon. Why do they keep ringing the doorbell like that?"

Papa stands up. He shuffles to the hall. "I'm coming, I'm coming," they hear him mutter. "And stop that ringing. It's driving me crazy."

"Maybe it's not the Germans," says Aunt Isabelle hopefully.

"May I come up?" a familiar voice calls.

"Hooray, it's Sander!" Rosa runs to the hall, and stands next to her father at the top of the steps. There is someone with Sander, a man carrying a black hat in his hand.

"Come on up, Sander!" Rosa shouts.

"I've brought a friend with me," says her uncle. "May he come, too?"

"Of course," Rosa answers, and she laughs. Sander can't just leave that man standing there, can he?

Sander leads the way up the stairs. The stranger follows. He bows to Father.

"My name is Goldstein," he says solemnly. "David Goldstein."

"I'm Herman de Jong." He extends his hand.

"Be careful," Sander warns Father. "Don't squeeze his hand too hard."

"Are you Rosa?" Mr. Goldstein asks, turning to her. "Fine, fine, that's what I thought. So *you* are the little... ouch...why are you pinching me, Sander?" he says, scowling at him.

He turns to Rosa again, and reaches toward her with both arms. "I'm Mr. Goldstein. It's a pleasure to meet you." He takes her hand very gently in his own. "I'm Mr. Goldstein," he repeats. "I see that we're about the same size."

Rosa pulls her hand away. What a strange little man that Mr. Goldstein is! And why did Papa have to be so careful when shaking his hand?

"Come, let's go inside," Father says. "Luckily, I don't have any coats to hang up, with this nice weather. Shall I put your hat on the hat rack, Mr. Goldstein?"

Mr. Goldstein clutches his hat to his chest. "No, thank you. I have to keep this hat close to me, always. But thank you, anyway."

"Rosa, is it all right if Mr. Goldstein sits in your chair?" asks Father. "And Sander, you take Silvie's chair. You girls have finished playing checkers, I think."

"We don't want to play when we have visitors here," says Rosa, and she smiles.

They have tea and punch to drink, and candy to eat. They talk about the war, and about the people who are in work camps. They also talk about the past, when they were allowed to visit anyone they wished, and when they were allowed to go by bicycle and by car.

"I used to have a wife and a son," says Mr. Goldstein. "I have only a son now. My wife died right before the war, and my son...ach, never mind." He puts his hands on his knees, and bows his head.

No one dares to say a word.

"What is that?" asks Mr. Goldstein, and he points to the floor. "I see a violin case. Under my chair. Whose is it?" He looks at Rosa.

"It's mine," Rosa answers.

"Yours? Can *you* play the violin?"

"Yes."

"And she plays very well, too," says Sander. Rosa notices that he is winking at Mr. Goldstein.

Mr. Goldstein stands up, and extends his hand to Rosa. "Then we're colleagues," he says, laughing. "I used to be the concertmaster of the Residentie Orchestra of The Hague. People had to be careful when shaking my hand then. I was always very careful with my hands, and I still am, out of habit. This is so nice, my dear. Will you play a little bit for me?"

Rosa takes her violin out of the case. "I'm afraid it's just going to be a children's song," she says.

She begins to play. Everyone listens attentively. She plays every children's song that she knows. When she has finished, she begins to play them all over again. When she finally puts her violin down, Mr. Goldstein is the first to applaud.

"That was beautiful," he says. "You play beautifully, my girl. I could tell you were good as soon as you started to play. Who is your teacher?"

"Mrs. Westen. But she can't teach me anymore. We're no longer allowed to go to the homes of non-Jews. And she can't come here for my lessons, because she broke her leg. She can't climb the stairs.

"Take a look," says Mr. Goldstein, and he points to his star. "Take a good look at this rotten thing."

Rosa looks at his star. What is there to see? What is so unusual about it?

"I can tell that you don't understand," he says. "Let me explain. You *are* allowed to come to my house. I'm Jewish. I wear a star, just like you."

"Don't you understand what Mr. Goldstein is trying to say?" Sander asks, and he walks toward Rosa. "Don't you understand that Mr. Goldstein wants to be your teacher? Wouldn't you like that?"

"I don't know yet."

"If you don't take lessons from him, you are the stupidest girl in Holland," Sander exclaims. "Haven't you ever heard of David Goldstein? Before the war began, didn't you ever see his face on a billboard?"

Rosa studies Mr. Goldstein's face carefully. "I've never seen him," she says at last.

"I haven't, either," says her mother.

Sander puts his hand over Mama's mouth. "I didn't ask *you*, big sister."

"You shouldn't force her," says Mr. Goldstein, winking at Sander. "If she doesn't want to study with me...maybe she'll be stuck playing those children's songs for the rest of her life. Maybe she'll never be able to play tunes by Beethoven and Bartók and the like."

"He is...he is...the most famous violinist..."

"Come on," says Mr. Goldstein, and he takes Sander by the hand. "Please stop it. You're embarrassing me."

"Maybe I *do* want to take lessons," Rosa blurts out.

"You have our permission," says Papa.

"Hooray!" Sander shouts. "My niece is going to take violin lessons again. When will you begin? Tomorrow? And when will there be a recital? You have other Jewish students, don't you, David?"

Mr. Goldstein nods. "I have a few more," he answers. "What do you think, Rosa? Shall we begin this week? How is Friday, at about three o'clock? Is that convenient for you?

My address is Eiklaan Number Seven. Don't bring your music books when you come. I want to listen to you first, and see exactly what you're capable of playing. All right?"

"Yes."

"Now go polish your violin. Phooey, just look at it. This is the first command from your new violin teacher. I'm very strict, you understand."

Rosa is no longer visiting with the others. She is polishing her violin. The scent of oil fills the room.

The violin begins to shine. Now and then she can catch a glimpse of her face on the varnish.

"You have a violin teacher again," she says to her reflection. "And you're allowed to go to his house because he's Jewish, just like you."

The girl on the violin smiles. Rosa smiles, too.

◆ Mr. Goldstein

Rosa is standing before the window in the living room. Why is the time passing so slowly today? This afternoon she will be going to Mr. Goldstein's house for her first lesson. Even though she is looking forward to it, there are moments when she has a sinking feeling at the bottom of her stomach.

Perhaps Mr. Goldstein will think that she is a terrible violinist now. "You'll never be able to play well," he will say, and will tell her not to come back again.

Rosa wishes that it were almost three o'clock, yet at the same time she doesn't; she is afraid to go to her lesson.

It is half past two. She walks up the stairs to fetch her violin from the bedroom. Philippe is lying in his crib. When he sees Rosa grasping her violin case, he stands up. He waves his hand as if he were conducting an orchestra. Rosa knows that this is his way of saying that he wants her to play for him.

"Not now, Philippe," she says. "Take your nap. I'm going to my violin lesson."

Philippe continues to wave.

"Go to sleep," she snaps. Rosa doesn't want to speak to Philippe in such a nasty tone of voice, but she can't help it.

Rosa walks down the Lindelaan. Just a little farther and she will be at Mr. Goldstein's house. The next street is the Eiklaan. She turns the corner, and stops in front of Number Seven.

Two nameplates are on the door.

GIDEON GOLDSTEIN — *Violinist*

is printed across the first one. On the second one it says:

MYRNA GOLDSTEIN-VAN PRAAG — *Pianist*
DAVID GOLDSTEIN — *Violinist*

"Rosa, is that you?" Mr. Goldstein is standing in the doorway. "I saw you coming, but it took so long for you to ring the bell that I thought, 'Come, I'd better look to see where that sweet girl is.' And now you're standing at the door. Were you afraid to ring the bell?"

"No, but it took me a while to read all those names on the door."

"Ach, I know, but I'm not taking the names off, not yet. Come in."

Rosa follows Mr. Goldstein. Their footsteps sound loud as they walk down the long marble hallway. He opens a door. They enter a large room filled with all kinds of chairs. Music books are scattered everywhere—on the floor, on the table, on the chairs. Dirty cups are lying everywhere, too. Rosa hardly dares to look around. Perhaps Mr. Goldstein would be embarrassed if he knew how startled she was by such untidiness.

"Beautiful, isn't it?" he says, walking toward a corner. "This is Myrna's piano," he says softly. "And look, there she is." He picks up a silver frame. Rosa sees the photograph of a woman with blond hair and blue eyes. She is wearing a blue dress.

"I have to put you back on your piano, Myrna," he says. "Rosa, did you know that a large piano such as this one is called a grand piano?"

"Of course. My grandpa and grandma in Groningen have one. No," she says, correcting herself, "they *had* one."

Mr. Goldstein doesn't seem to hear her. He takes a red velvet cloth from the pocket of his trousers, and begins to wipe the piano. "I dust the piano every day," he explains. "When Gideon returns from the work camp, he'll be playing it. I've received word from him that he's in Mauthausen, and that he's doing fine."

"On the door outside it says that Gideon is a violinist."

"That's true, but he plays the piano beautifully, as well." Mr. Goldstein strokes the piano. "Come," he says. "You're here for your first violin lesson. Shall we begin? Take out your violin."

"All right."

"Play what you want."

Rosa stands up very straight, just as Mrs. Westen taught her to do. She closes her eyes, to better hear the music that is going through her head. She begins to play her violin. She plays the songs that she always plays for Philippe, adding trills to make them sound even prettier. The tunes roll first through her head, then out the violin.

"May I play with you?" Mr. Goldstein asks. "You just carry on. I'll do the accompaniment. I'll play the same song as you, but it will sound a bit different. Don't let my part confuse you. Have you ever played with someone else before?"

"Yes, with Uncle Louis on the piano. We played a concertino by Rieding. And I've played with Mrs. Westen, of course."

"Fine, then let's go ahead. You begin."

Rosa plays a couple of notes. Mr. Goldstein joins in, too. How wonderful it sounds! They play song after song. Suddenly, Mr. Goldstein stops. He glances at his watch.

"Unbelievable," he says. "It's already four-thirty. Time flies when you enjoy what you're doing. I'll give you a glass of punch, and then you'll have to go home. I'll see you next Friday. Do you want to play children's songs at your next lesson?"

"No, I don't want to play children's songs anymore."

"All right. Then I have an idea. I'll give you a sheet of music to take home. I've written all the notes out for you. Practice this piece carefully. When you return next week,

I'll tell you a little bit about the music. I won't say anything more now. Let me give you some punch. Come with me to the kitchen. I have something to show you, something you've never seen before. Come on."

Mr. Goldstein leads the way to the kitchen. "Come on," he repeats. "You don't have to be afraid of me. Here, take a glass. Hold it under the tap."

Rosa does as she is told. Mr. Goldstein turns on the faucet. "Take a look. Here comes the punch!" he calls. "I have a magic tap, you see. Green punch flows out of it."

Rosa looks wide-eyed at her glass. It is filled with a green liquid now.

"Taste it," he says. "I'm not going to tell you anything about that magic tap. Not even Gideon knows how it works, and he is twenty-four years old. Maybe when he comes back from Mauthausen, I'll tell him how it works. And then I'll tell you, too."

Rosa hardly dares to drink the green stuff. It might be poison. Perhaps Mr. Goldstein is a wicked little elf.

"Don't be afraid to drink it. It's not poisonous. Wait, I'll have a glass, too. Maybe you'll trust me then."

Rosa is startled. Mr. Goldstein must be a mind reader. She takes a small sip. "It tastes like plums," she says.

"That's right. It's plum punch. Delicious, isn't it?"

Rosa takes another sip, and another, until her glass is empty.

"Was it good?" he asks.

"Mmmm."

"It's time for you to go home. And I'm going to make myself a sandwich. Before Gideon was deported, he cooked supper for the two of us. I just have a sandwich in the evenings now."

"I'm…I'm leaving." Rosa doesn't want Mr. Goldstein to know that she wants to go home. He seems to be so very lonely.

"I'm already looking forward to next Friday," he says. "And I think that you play quite well. I'm glad that Sander thought of that trick to get you—"

"Trick? What trick?"

Mr. Goldstein slaps his forehead. "What a fool I am. Now I've told you everything. Now you know that Sander brought me to your house on purpose, to try to make you want to take lessons from me. Please don't tell anyone about this, Rosa. Artists like you and me are very absent-minded sometimes. We often have trouble fibbing."

"I know. And I'm glad that you want to be my teacher."

"Then all is well. Do you know what we'll do? When you become a truly fine violinist, we'll give a recital with Gideon, after the war. There is plenty of music written for two violins and piano. We'll rent an auditorium, and perform there. You will wear a long blue dress, and Gideon and I will wear jackets with long coattails, and bow ties. I think Gideon might even wear his hat. That strange boy claims that he can play the piano well only when he has on that black hat. He forgot to take it with him when he went to the work camp. I'm so afraid of losing it that I always want to keep it close to me. Look, there it is, on that chair over there."

Rosa looks at the chair that Mr. Goldstein is pointing to, but she doesn't see anything.

"I must have put something on top of it," he says. "Yes, this week's *The Jewish Weekly*." He picks up the newspaper, and throws it on the floor. Rosa can see the hat now.

"Do you know what worries me a little?" he asks. "Gideon's hands. When he comes back, I want him to be able to play the violin again, and that—"

"I've got to go home. It's already quarter after five."

"Yes, of course. I talk too much. All people who live alone do that. Excuse me. Come, I'll let you out."

Rosa picks up her violin and the sheet of music. Together they walk to the door.

"Hurry home," he says. "See you next week."

"Goodbye, sir, see you next week."

"If the good Lord is willing," Mr. Goldstein calls to her. "And stay well, my girl!"

Rosa turns around. Mr. Goldstein is still standing in the doorway. She doesn't want to look at him now. He seems to be so very lonely.

◆ *Wunderkind*

Rosa is angry with Mr. Goldstein. As soon as she returned from her first lesson, she set the new piece on her music stand. She was planning to practice it very hard, so that at her next lesson she would play it without making any mistakes. But as she looked at the notes, she could tell right away that the piece was much too easy for her. She was playing this kind of music two years ago! Doesn't Mr. Goldstein know that she can already play pieces that are very complicated, *so* complicated that Lita Rosa calls her a *wunderkind*? Or are the pieces by Rieding and Fiocco not complicated?

"He didn't want to make it too difficult for you this first time," Mama said to her.

"He didn't want to discourage you," said Aunt Isabelle.

Their words have no effect. Rosa remains angry. "I'll go one more time," she grumbled. "And if he gives me another babyish piece to play, he'll never see *me* again."

It is already Friday. The day is passing much more quickly than it did a week ago. Rosa is ready to go to Mr. Goldstein's house. She has stuffed the music sheet into her pocket. She will tell her teacher that she is too advanced for this stupid piece. If Mr. Goldstein *really* wants to hear it, she will play it one more time. After that, she will throw it in the garbage can.

Rosa walks down the street. She would love to go to the beach some afternoon, just as she used to do. She would dig a hole in the sand so deep that water would seep into it. She would keep digging until she was practically in Australia! She would no longer be afraid if her cousins buried her in the sand, for she is old enough to know that she can't suffocate as long as she keeps her nose above the ground.

Rosa doesn't want to think about the past anymore; it makes her feel so unhappy.

"Here she is!"

Rosa doesn't need to ring the bell. Mr. Goldstein is waiting for her at the door. He has probably been standing there a long time.

"I'm glad you're here," he says. "Did you practice hard?"

"Mmmm."

"Do you like the piece?"

"It's all right."

"Too difficult, perhaps? Ach, those children's songs are much easier."

Rosa doesn't answer.

"Wait until you see the room. You won't believe your eyes. Come." Mr. Goldstein steps inside. "Come into my palace," he says, and he laughs. "I was about to ask you to take your shoes off."

They enter the room. At first it looks the same as it did last week. Suddenly, Rosa can see a tremendous change. There is not a single book or newspaper or dirty cup lying about; Mr. Goldstein has cleared everything away.

"I cleaned the room just for you, because I was so happy that you were coming," he says.

"It looks much better," says Rosa.

"And now we'll begin." Mr. Goldstein lays a sheet of music on the table. "Have you ever seen this piece in a music book?" he asks.

"It's almost the same as this..." Rosa lifts up her skirt, and takes the crumbled paper from her pocket.

"Phooey, how sloppy," he exclaims. "Yes, this is the accompaniment to 'Waltz of the Clouds,' the piece you've been practicing. And here comes my surprise. Who do you think composed it?"

Rosa ponders a moment before answering. "Mozart?" she says.

"Wrong."

"Haydn?"

"Wrong. I'll tell you: Gideon is the composer. He wrote it when he was just about your age."

Rosa blushes. "How clever of him," she says.

"Shall we begin now?" Mr. Goldstein sits down in a chair. He closes his eyes. "Start playing the waltz," he says. "If there is something I want to correct, I'll tap against the table. But I don't think I'll need to say very much. You've practiced diligently, of course."

Rosa begins to play. It is going well. Why shouldn't it? It is such an easy piece!

There is a tap on the table. "That third measure has to be much softer, and make sure you play the trill in the fourth measure. And don't forget to use vibrato, please."

Rosa keeps playing. How strict Mr. Goldstein is! He begins to sing along.

"And...up-bow...and down-bow...and loud now...yes, forte...and stop!"

Rosa almost drops her bow.

"Come sit next to me at the table."

Slowly she walks to a chair across from him.

"No, close to me." Mr. Goldstein pulls out the chair next to him. "Sit down," he says. He puts his hand on her shoulder. "Look deep into my trusty brown eyes. You didn't practice, did you?"

"No," Rosa whispers.

"Much too easy, is it? Child prodigies don't have to practice, do they? Sander tells me that your Aunt Lita Rosa calls you a *wunderkind*. Don't let it go to your head, my girl. Just practice hard. Even the so-called easy pieces."

Rosa doesn't know what to say. Fortunately, Mr. Goldstein laughs.

"And now we'll play the waltz together," he says. He takes his violin, and sits down next to Rosa. "We're just like two musical dwarfs," he says with a chuckle. "And I'm quite a rascal, don't you think?"

"One, two, three. One, two, three," she counts.

"Good!" he calls. "Keep going. You're doing fine!"

Rosa never dreamed that the little tune written on the scrap of paper could sound so beautiful.

"Next week, if you can play 'Waltz of the Clouds' like a true *wunderkind*, we'll play a duet by Bartók, the two of us together," he says. "If you like the music, that is. It's very modern."

"I'm not a *wunderkind*."

"But I can tease you a little bit, can't I?"

"Yes."

"Listen. I'm going to play something for you, and I want to know what you think of it." Mr. Goldstein places a music book on a wooden stand. The sound of high notes reverberates through the room.

"It's pretty," she says. "A little weird, but pretty."

"That was by Bartók. We'll play it together next week if..."

"If I've practiced Gideon's waltz."

"Sit down. Here, in this chair." Mr. Goldstein sits down next to her. "Do you have any idea why I want your lesson to be on Friday afternoon?"

"No."

"You know, of course, that Saturday is *Shabbes*, our day of rest. And that the *Shabbes* begins on Friday, late in the afternoon."

"Of course I know that. I'm Jewish, too."

"I always feel terribly alone on Friday. But when you come for your lesson on Friday afternoon, in the evening I don't feel the loneliness so much. When my wife was alive, she lighted the *Shabbes* candles. You know that it is customary for the woman of the house to do this. After she died, Gideon and I continued to light the candles. I don't do it anymore now. Will you stay and have dinner with me, on a Friday afternoon? Then *you* may light the candles. *You* are a bit of a woman, after all."

"I can't," Rosa answers. "I want to be home on Friday evening. But you can have dinner with us, can't you? We have wonderful food on Fridays, chicken and applesauce and soup. And after we eat, we play games."

"Never mind. Let's wait awhile. Your mother is busy enough with all those people in the house. And I'm also afraid that I won't be back home by eight o'clock. Later on, perhaps, I'll have dinner at your house. Well, I've complained enough. What kind of a violin teacher am I? It's already quarter past four. Have some punch, then home you go. Here is your glass."

Green punch flows from the tap, just as it did the week before. "You know what I said," he reminds her. "I'll tell you the secret of the plum punch when Gideon comes home."

Rosa begins to drink. The green stuff is very tasty. She sets her empty glass in the sink.

"I'm going to wash the dishes as soon as you leave," says Mr. Goldstein. "I never want to have such a mess in the house again."

He leads Rosa to the door, and kisses her gently on her forehead.

She walks down the street. When she is almost at the

corner, she hears him calling, "See you next week. Practice hard, and stay well!"

"You, too!" Rosa shouts. She takes a few steps, then turns around to wave to her teacher.

The door is closed.

◆ Taking a Walk

"Stop it, Philippe! Don't pull on my shoelace like that. I've got to practice. It's almost Friday, and I have to be able to play 'Waltz of the Clouds' without making any mistakes. Otherwise I can't start the Bartók duet."

Rosa carries Philippe to another corner of the room, but it's no use. He has crawled back to her before she has scarcely played four measures. He sits at her feet, and tugs on her left shoelace.

"Stop that, Philippe!" she shouts.

"What's going on in here?" Aunt Isabelle has entered the living room.

"I can't practice because Philippe is bothering me," Rosa complains. "And I have to learn Gideon's piece by Friday."

"You mean the little waltz that is actually too easy for you?" Aunt Isabelle asks.

"It's not easy."

"Oh, but last week..."

"Philippe!" Rosa bellows. Her right shoelace is now loose, as well.

"Rosa, would you like to do me a favor?" Aunt Isabelle asks, looking very earnest.

"Hmmm."

"Would you take Philippe for a little walk? I'm terribly tired. He'll go to bed when you come back, and then you can practice without being disturbed. Silvie is upstairs. Shall I ask her to go with you?"

Rosa nods. She doesn't really want to take a walk. She wants to practice. But she can see that Aunt Isabelle is very tired indeed. Her cheeks are pale, and it is obvious that she stopped bleaching her mustache long ago. Perhaps she has been staying indoors so much lately because she doesn't look as pretty as she used to. Perhaps that is also the reason she doesn't want to go outside with Philippe now.

"Silvie, will you take Philippe for a walk?" Rosa hears Aunt Isabelle call.

"Yes, I'm coming!" Silvie runs downstairs. "Are you going, too?" she asks Rosa.

"Yes."

"I'll bring Philippe downstairs," says Aunt Isabelle. "Come, Philippe, Rosa and Silvie are taking you for a walk." She lifts him up. "Goodness, you're getting to be so heavy," she exclaims.

"Where shall we go?" asks Rosa.

"To the shops along the Herenstraat," Silvie replies.

"But we can't go inside," says Rosa. "You know that, don't you?"

"Of course I know that. We can go in only between three and five o'clock. I just want to look at the display windows. Can we go now? And may I push the stroller?"

They walk in the sun. Philippe points to all the things he likes.

"Tam...tam!" he calls, pointing to the tram.

"We can't, Philippe," says Silvie. "We're not allowed to ride in it. But when the war is over, we'll spend an entire day riding the tram with you. That's what we'll do, won't we, Rosa?"

"Yes, that's what we'll do," her sister agrees. "We'll pack sandwiches for ourselves, and we'll bring along a bottle of milk for Philippe."

"Look over there," Silvie exclaims, pointing in the distance. "Soldiers! I want to go home. They're coming toward us."

"Just keep walking." Rosa grabs Silvie by her blouse. "Those soldiers are marching. They're not rounding up anybody."

The soldiers are coming closer. The girls can hear the clicking of their heels against the road. Philippe sits straight up in his stroller. He sways back and forth, just as he always does when he hears music.

"No!" Rosa puts her hands over her ears. "Now they're starting to sing, too. I can't stand it. Come on, let's go down the Bilderdijklaan. Maybe we won't hear them there."

They duck into the side street, but there is no getting away from it; the soldiers are singing very loudly.

"They're singing about us," Silvie cries.

"They're singing 'Judenblut en Messer,'" Rosa whispers. "I think that means 'Jewish blood and knives.'"

Philippe claps his hands to the beat of the music. Bubbles are pouring from his mouth. He laughs. The singing grows softer as the soldiers disappear down the street.

Philippe begins to cry.

"Stupid boy," says Silvie. "Stop crying. I want to go home."

"So do I. I want to practice, but we can't go back yet."

"Why not?"

"Philippe isn't tired enough to go to sleep. Let's go look at the display windows on the Herenstraat."

They walk past the Magneet. They walk past the Sierkan, and past Torica.

"Papa bought his glasses there," says Rosa, pointing. "I think that I'll have to get glasses too, after the war. I don't want them now, because everyone would call me 'four-eyed Jew.' But I won't mind getting them when I no longer have to wear a star."

They stop in front of the Old Church, across from the police station. "Look, there is Sander's studio," says Silvie, pointing to the Kerklaan. "I'd like to go there again sometime. It's been a while since we visited him. We haven't been there since his birthday, and that was in April. Do you think it's all right to sit on the fence by the church, Rosa?"

"No, I don't think so," Rosa shades her eyes with her hand. "I think I see soldiers coming again. I can see a long line of people. But I don't hear any music, and they're not singing, either."

She squints a little. "They're not soldiers," she says, after a moment. "They're ordinary people. They're coming closer."

"I see children in the line, too," Silvie whispers. "They have stars on their clothes, and they're carrying rucksacks. Here they come. They must have been caught in a roundup. A policeman is walking in front of them, and another policeman is walking behind them."

"Quick, turn around," Rosa whispers. "If the policemen see our stars, we'll have to join the group, too."

The girls stand with their backs to the police station. Philippe doesn't have to turn around, for he is too young to be wearing a star.

"Let's pretend that we're looking at the church," says Rosa.

"What a pretty steeple!" Silvie calls, as loud as she can. "And what lovely green grass. And what a beautiful water pump!"

Rosa looks behind her. An officer pushes a few of the children into the station.

"Let's go home," she says.

They walk back down the Herenstraat, and cross the street where the soldiers were marching just moments before. Philippe is sleeping. His hands are hanging over the side of the stroller. His mouth is open, and his head is drooping a little.

"Where do you think those people will be going?" Silvie asks.

"To Westerbork, I think, just like Clary and Freddy and Mr. Nuszbaum," Rosa answers. "All Jews who are arrested go to Westerbork first."

"Will we go to Westerbork, too?"

"I don't know. Maybe we will."

"I don't want to," says Silvie.

"I don't want to, either."

When the girls are home again, Aunt Isabelle asks, "Did Philippe behave himself? Did he have a good time?"

"I think so," Rosa answers. "*He* is little."

"And what about you? Did you girls have a good time, too?"

"We saw soldiers," says Silvie, "and they were singing. And we..."

Rosa runs out of the room. She returns with her violin. "I have to practice," she says. "You'll have to stop talking now."

The sound of Gideon's waltz fills the room.

◆ Surprise

Rosa is certain that Mr. Goldstein will be pleased when he hears her play "Waltz of the Clouds" today. She has practiced Gideon's piece very thoroughly. She is looking forward to her lesson, for she will be allowed to begin the Bartók now. She is so excited that she skips all the way to her teacher's house.

"How nice and early you are." Mr. Goldstein is waiting for her at the door. "I'm glad you're here. Come right in."

Rosa begins to walk down the hall.

"No," he says. "Your lesson will be upstairs today."

They climb a long stairway. Mr. Goldstein opens a door. "We'll work in here today," he says. "This is Gideon's room. Put the waltz on his music stand."

Rosa takes the sheet out of her pocket. It doesn't look as crumpled as it did last week, because she has ironed it with Mama's iron.

"That's much better," he remarks. "The paper isn't wadded up anymore. Take out your violin. I have a feeling that you practiced diligently this week."

Rosa begins to play. Mr. Goldstein closes his eyes. He moves his whole body to the beat of the music as he hums the tune. It seems as though he and the violin are singing the melody together.

The waltz is over. Mr. Goldstein is still sitting with his eyes closed. Rosa hardly dares to move. It looks as though he is sleeping. She coughs, but he remains motionless. Rosa is becoming a bit frightened. Perhaps Mr. Goldstein is dead. She coughs again. He opens his eyes. "Will you play it once more?" he asks.

Rosa begins the piece again. Mr. Goldstein is listening with his eyes open now. He applauds when she has finished.

"Splendid," he says. "That was beautiful. And now that I've heard you play the waltz, I'm starting to think that Gideon was a *wunderkind*, too."

Rosa begins to laugh. "I think you're right," she says. "Are we going to play Bartók now?"

"No, not 'we.' I'll play a piece for you first, to show you how it sounds. And if you practice it very carefully, we'll play it together next week. Here is the music."

He hands her a book. "Forty-four Violin Duos by Béla Bartók" is printed across the front. Rosa opens it.

"It's so difficult!" she exclaims in alarm. "I'll never be able to play this."

"Practice hard," says Mr. Goldstein. "It will sound strange for a while, but as you become used to it, you'll discover how beautiful modern music can be. I'll show you."

He begins to play, slowly at first, then a bit faster. The

notes seem to be all jumbled together. Rosa has never heard music like this before. It hurts her ears a little, but Mr. Goldstein keeps playing. Why doesn't he stop?

"That's enough now," he says, when he has finished. "How do you like it?"

"It's very pretty."

"I thought you would like it, even though I saw you making a face every now and then, just as you did when I played the Bartók at your last lesson. Take the book home, and practice it carefully this week. You have no idea what the music will sound like when we play it together.

"And now I have a surprise," he continues. "Your lesson is over, and you are coming downstairs with me. What time is it?"

"Quarter to four."

"Fine. We'll have time to eat a Sabbath dinner together."

"I can't. I have to be home by six o'clock."

Mr. Goldstein begins to laugh secretively. "Come downstairs, and you'll understand why I want so much for you to stay," he says.

They walk down the long stairway. Mr. Goldstein stops in front of the kitchen door. "Come," he whispers. "The surprise is in here."

They enter the kitchen. "Look inside the pans," he says. "Soup and chicken and applesauce. All for you. Will you stay?"

"All right," says Rosa, and she sighs.

"Come, then, let's begin our dinner."

Rosa follows Mr. Goldstein into the dining room. "Nice, isn't it? Sit down." He points to the table, which is decked in a white cloth. Two flowered plates have been placed on it, and two wine glasses, one large and one small. Many serving spoons have been set on the table, as well.

"Sit down," he repeats. "Don't worry. I'll make sure that you are home on time. I'll get the soup from the kitchen now."

Rosa gazes around the room. On the piano is a vase filled with red roses. The spoons and forks gleam on the table, and the crystal lamp reflects a thousand colors above her.

Mr. Goldstein returns, and lays the soup bowls on the table. "You may light the *Shabbes* candles," he says, and places two white candles in front of her. "Here are the matches."

Rosa lights the candles. Her hands are trembling a little.

"*Gut Shabbes*," he says.

"Yes, and a good Sabbath to you, too," she replies.

They begin their meal. "Well, how is it?" he asks, looking at Rosa expectantly.

"It's delicious. I love vermicelli soup."

"I'll get the rest of our dinner." Mr. Goldstein goes into the kitchen, and brings back three platters. He places them in the middle of the table. The steam rises from the food, all the way up to the lamp above. The room is growing warm. Rosa can hardly take her eyes off her teacher, for she has never seen him like this before. He looks so very happy.

They eat, and they talk. They drink the sweet wine. "Gideon gave me this wine," he tells her.

Rosa wishes that Mr. Goldstein would not talk about Gideon. Whenever he does, a wave of sadness seems to come over him.

"It's time for our dessert. Will you fetch it from the kitchen? It's right by the sink."

"Of course." Rosa is already on her way. She enters the kitchen, and finds the two dessert dishes. In each one is a small paper parasol, and under each parasol is a thick pink pudding.

She looks at the dessert in dismay. She can't stand thick pudding; eating it always makes her feel sick. She places the bowls on a tray, and carries the tray down the hall. The bowls slide around a bit. *Shall I drop the tray?* she wonders. *No, I'd better not.*

Rosa manages to swallow some of the pudding, even though she can barely keep from gagging on it.

"Take my parasol," says Mr. Goldstein. "You can give it to Philippe later, when you get home. What am I saying, 'later'? You have to go home now. It's already five-thirty. Thank you for sharing a wonderful, old-fashioned Friday evening with me. Here, quickly…take the Bartók duets, and the parasol for Philippe. I'll bring you to the door, as usual."

Mr. Goldstein opens the front door. "Did you notice it was pouring down rain outside?" he asks.

"No, not at all."

"That's because we were having such a nice time together. When—"

"I've got to hurry. I don't want to be late."

"Wait a minute." He runs up the stairs, and returns with Gideon's hat. "Wear this," he pants. "It will keep your hair dry. Your hair will lose its lovely curl if it gets wet."

Rosa would like to say that her hair won't lose its curl because it is naturally curly, but she puts on the hat without saying a word.

"It looks nice on you," he whispers. "Don't forget to bring it back next week. And something else you mustn't forget: A beautifully practiced Bartók. If you *can* practice, that is."

"What do you mean?" Rosa doesn't understand how Mr. Goldstein knows that Philippe bothers her sometimes when she practices. She has never told him about it.

He bursts out laughing. "Your violin, sweetheart...upstairs in Gideon's room."

Rosa dashes up the steps. She snatches her violin from Gideon's bed, and runs back down again.

"Goodbye, Mr. Goldstein," she says, gasping. "Thank you very much for everything." She catches her breath a little. "You should go in the house now; it's much too wet and windy to stand outside and wave to me."

Rosa begins to run. She hears the door close behind her. She must hurry, for it is already five minutes to six. It is difficult to run, for the wind is very strong. She stops. She has a pain in her side, a terrible, stabbing sensation that her parents call "growing pains."

The wind blows the hat from her head. Rosa chases it. She must not lose that hat; if she does, Gideon will never be able to play the piano when he returns. She keeps running. She almost has it. She steps on the rim. The hat can't blow any farther now. She has beaten the wind!

Rosa continues to run. She ignores the pain in her side.

At quarter after six she is standing in front of her door. Now she will be able to tell her family all about Mr. Goldstein, and about the wind, too.

"You're late," says Papa. "If it weren't for the war, I would send you to bed without your supper."

"I don't want any supper. I'm not hungry," says Rosa.

She enters the living room. Mama begins to light the candles. "We wanted to wait for you, Rosa," she says.

"*Gut Shabbes!*" everyone calls all at once. "A very good *Shabbes!*"

Suddenly, Rosa begins to cry. She cries about Mr. Goldstein, because he is so alone now. She cries about the candles, and she cries about the war. And why doesn't anyone ask her about Gideon's hat? Why doesn't anyone ask if Mr. Goldstein was pleased with her lesson, or whether she may play Bartók now?

Something terrible must have happened again today. Whenever grown-ups receive bad news, they don't pay much attention to children.

"What happened? Have more people been arrested? What horrible things have been reported in the Jewish newspaper today?" she should ask.

Rosa doesn't say a word. She cries, and she is angry with herself for doing so. She brushes her hand against her cheek.

"Here, take this," says Uncle Louis, putting a handkerchief in her hand.

Rosa wipes away her tears. She blows her nose. "I'm all right now," she whispers. "A good Sabbath to you, Uncle Louis."

"*Gut Shabbes*, Rosa," he replies.

◆ *Pneumonia*

"You'll have to bundle up when you go to Mr. Goldstein's house this afternoon," says Father. "It seems as though it will never be dry again. It's been raining for almost a week now."

With his finger he traces the path of a drop of water as it drips down the window. "I'm glad you'll be able to show Mr. Goldstein how well you've practiced," he continues. "I've heard that piece by Bartók so much that I'm sick of it. I know it practically from memory. Maybe you can take on a different composer next week."

Rosa bursts out laughing. She can well imagine why Papa is talking this way. She has probably played the Bartók a hundred times, and it sounded so awful at first that even *she* found it shocking. It is a very difficult piece, but Mr. Goldstein said that a child like her should be able to learn it. She is looking forward to playing the duet with her teacher, even though she is a bit afraid that it won't go very well. Perhaps her hands will shake so much that she will drop her bow. Perhaps she will play all the notes out of tune.

"Here comes the mailman with *The Jewish Weekly*," says Papa, and he taps against the window. "Let's see what sort of misery the newspaper will be describing for us today." He shuffles out of the room. Rosa can hear him walking slowly down the stairs.

"It's soaked." Papa lays the newspaper on the table. "I can hardly read it," he complains. "What a sloppy mailman we have. I'm going to report him to the post office."

Very carefully he turns a page, then another.

"It's funny that a wet newspaper doesn't rustle, isn't it, Papa?" says Rosa. "Don't tear it."

Her father doesn't answer. He crouches even lower over the table. "Oh, no!" he calls. "That can't be. Rosa, that *can't* be!"

"What's the matter?" Rosa bends over the paper, too.

"Here, by my finger. Read it."

She reads the words that are printed between two black lines:

We were just informed of the death of our dear son
Donald
He reached the age of twenty-one years
He died of pneumonia in Mauthausen

His grieving parents:
Jacques Bohemen
Tiny Bohemen-van Dam
Amsterdam, September 1942

"This is dreadful, too," says Father. He points to another death notice:

Some months ago, our only son and brother
Benno
passed away at the age of nineteen
He died of pneumonia in Mauthausen

M. Groen
D. Groen-Visraper
Anita

"In Mauthausen," Rosa whispers. "Gideon is in Mauthausen, too."

Father begins to pace back and forth. "They've only just notified the families," he says, nearly in tears. "First the uncertainty for the parents, and now the truth. How cruel the Germans are!"

"There is a sister mentioned in the second notice," says Rosa softly.

"And don't think for a moment that they died of pneumonia," says Father. "They were murdered, and we'll be murdered, too. All of us."

"Stop it, Papa."

"Am I scaring you?"

"Yes. You scare me all the time."

"I won't say anything more. I'll keep my mouth shut. You're right. You are much too young for all this grief. I'll have to be more careful."

He paces the floor in silence. It seems as though his back is becoming even more bent.

"Mr. Goldstein gets *The Jewish Weekly*, too," says Rosa. "I don't want him to see those death notices."

Her father stops pacing. "I don't know what you can do about it," he exclaims.

"I don't, either," she says. "Maybe the mailman who delivers on the Eiklaan will have an accident, or something. Maybe he'll drop his mailbag into a puddle, and all the newspapers and letters will get wet."

"It's time for you to go," says Father. "It's already two-thirty."

Rosa puts on Gideon's hat, and steps out the door. She clutches her violin case to her chest; she wants to protect her instrument from the rain, which is coming down harder than ever. She doesn't feel like going to Mr. Goldstein's house now. She hopes that he hasn't seen those dreary death notices. He is already so worried about his son; what will he do if he reads about the fate of those other young men?

Rosa is getting a terrible stomachache. It is so bad that she is doubled over in pain. Should she go home?

Suddenly, she has an idea. She begins to walk upright again. If she jumps in the puddles, her boots will become covered with mud. "My boots are filthy," she will tell Mr. Goldstein. "I'll have to take them off, and I'll need a newspaper to set them down on. I'll get the paper myself." Naturally, she will take today's paper, and will make it so dirty that he won't be able to read a single word.

Rosa skips through the puddles. She holds her violin case high above her head, for she doesn't want mud to splatter on it.

She is already at the Lindelaan. Just a little further, and she will be at her teacher's house.

Mr. Goldstein is not standing outside today. It's no wonder, because it is still pouring down rain.

When she reaches for the bell, she sees something unusual on the door. It looks like a postage stamp, but it is much larger, and bright red. An eagle is printed on it, and a German word, too. Rosa knows what that stamp means; she has seen it many times on the homes of people who have been deported.

"No!" she shouts. "Open the door, Mr. Goldstein! Hurry! It's me, Rosa!"

The door remains closed. She looks through the mail slot, and sees a pile of letters on the doormat.

Mr. Goldstein is gone. The Germans have taken him away. What is she to do?

Rosa stands motionless in front of the door. She tries to read the word on the stamp, but she can't. Drops of rain roll down her cheeks. She never knew that rain could taste so salty.

She turns around. Slowly she walks back down the Linde-laan. She is no longer holding her violin to her chest. The wind lifts the hat off her head, but Rosa continues on her way.

"Please, God, blow Gideon's hat toward the East," she prays.

God is not answering her prayers today.

◆ *Dreaming*

Philippe is walking! He is so proud that after taking a couple of steps, he sits on the floor and claps his hands.

With much groaning he stands up, runs away, sits down, claps his hands, stands up…

"Rosa, aren't you proud of Philippe?" Aunt Isabelle asks. "Yes."

"Then clap for him, like the rest of us."

Rosa doesn't move. She is curled up in the big chair. She wants only to sit and think about Mr. Goldstein. Sometimes it seems as though he is in the room. She can hear him talking to her, and if she listens very carefully, she can hear him playing the violin, too. The sound of music rises above the talking of the others. He has a glass of green punch in his hand.

"I can no longer show you how I get this green punch to come out of my kitchen tap," he says. "But I'll reveal the secret of that magic tap when Gideon and I return."

He is standing in a circle of light. "Will you open the window for me?" he asks. "I want to leave now."

Rosa climbs out of the chair. She walks to the window, and raises it up high.

"Don't!" Uncle Louis pulls on her sleeve. "Look out. Philippe might stand on a chair near that window one day, and then he would fall out."

Uncle Louis closes the window.

Mr. Goldstein is no longer in the room. Rosa hears violin music outside. She presses her face against the window pane, and sees him on a roof, across the street from their house. He is wearing Gideon's hat, and is playing the violin more beautifully than she has ever heard him play before. All the notes are high and pure. A bird is flying above his head. To his left, eight white candles are burning, and a woman in a long blue dress is floating above him.

146

"Mr. Goldstein! Hello, Mr. Goldstein! Here I am!" calls Rosa, and she waves.

She continues to stare out the window, for Mr. Goldstein is still on the roof. The white candles are burning, and the woman is floating high above his head.

Rosa doesn't want to eat, and she doesn't want to drink. She wants only to stand before the window, nothing more. If she steps away, Mr. Goldstein might leave, too, and never come back. Never.

She is being picked up. Someone is holding her stiffly in his arms. Rosa can tell by the smell of paint that it is Uncle Louis who is carrying her out of the room.

"I'm putting you to bed," he says. "You're sick with grief."

"Mr. Goldstein!" she screams.

"Not so wild," says Uncle Louis, as he carries her up the stairs. "If you thrash around like that, I'll drop you. Ow, what are you doing? Why are you biting my nose? Have you lost your mind?" He throws her onto her bed, and runs out of the room.

"She really is *crazy!*" Rosa hears him call. "She bit me on the nose, that vicious girl. I think I'm bleeding."

Let the grown-ups believe that she is crazy. She doesn't care. She wants to sleep now; she won't leave her bed until the war is over. She doesn't need to eat, and she doesn't need to drink.

"Mr. Goldstein! I'm not crazy, am I? Tell me I'm not crazy!"

"Rosa, come out from under the covers." Father's voice. She doesn't move.

"Leave her alone." Another man's voice. "Don't force her."

"Rosa!" Mama's voice.

"What are we doing now, my girl? Don't we feel like getting out of bed?" The other man's voice again.

"What should we do, doctor?" Papa's voice sounds frightened.

"I'd like to introduce myself, even if you don't want to see me, Rosa," says the stranger. "I'm Dr. Simons. I'm a child psychiatrist. Your father has just been by to see me, and to ask me to help you. I know a lot about children's souls, and I have a very weird appearance. Would you like to know how weird?"

"No."

"What are you so unhappy about?"

"Nothing."

"Everything?"

"Yes."

"She has had a terrible shock. That much is obvious." The stranger is speaking in a very low voice now. "I don't want to do anything more today. If she is not better by tomorrow, I'll come back. I'm leaving some valerian drops with you. Try to give them to her in a small spoon. They will calm her, and perhaps during the course of the day..."

Rosa cannot hear the rest, for the man is speaking very quietly. She hears the three of them go down the stairs.

"Mr. Goldstein!" She slams her fists into her pillow. "Damn! Damn you all!"

"What is the matter? Do you need me, Rosa?"

Mr. Goldstein is standing next to her. He sets his rucksack on the floor, and sits down on Silvie's bed. "Why are you calling me?"

"I don't want you to go East."

"Why not?"

"I want you to stay here."

"No, I have to go. I'll be joining Gideon. It's a shame that I don't have his hat. He'll be cold. In two months it will be winter."

"I can't help it, Mr. Goldstein. The wind lifted the hat from my head, and blew it away." Rosa begins to cry.

Mr. Goldstein puts his arm around her. He begins to hum Gideon's waltz. Rosa hums the waltz with him. He stands up, takes his violin out of his rucksack, and begins to play.

"Shall I get my violin out, too?" she asks. "It's under my bed."

They play a duet together. The music is so beautiful that it gives her goose bumps.

"Béla Bartók should be very pleased," says Mr. Goldstein. "That was lovely, wasn't it?"

Rosa stops playing. Mr. Goldstein is no longer standing on the floor. He is floating toward the light on the ceiling. He floats to the window, and taps the pane with his bow.

"Don't leave!" she shouts. "Don't leave me, Mr. Goldstein!"

She bites her hand. She pounds on her pillow. "No!" she shouts.

"Rosa!" She hears Sander's voice in her room. "Come out from under the covers, Rosa."

"No!"

"I think that you're being a bit egotistical."

"Egotistical?" She pulls the covers to the side a little. "What do you mean, egotistical?"

"You're thinking only of yourself. Are *you* the only person in this house who is unhappy? Haven't you noticed how your parents feel? How Isabelle and Louis feel? How *I* feel? David Goldstein was my friend, too."

Rosa pulls her covers a bit farther aside. "They're sending him to Poland. Papa said that we'll all be going there. And I don't want to go to Poland!" She turns over onto her stomach, and begins to pound on her pillow again. "I don't want to. I don't want to!"

"Come sit on my lap. I'll try to comfort you. I'll sing songs for you, as many as you want." He wraps his arms around her, and begins to sing:

> *Sleep, baby, sleep,*
> *Outside there roams a sheep,*
> *A sheep...*

"I can feel your heart beating," says Rosa. "It's under my ear."

He continues to sing. Rosa puts her thumb in her mouth. She would like to sit in Sander's lap forever.

He whispers something in her ear. At first she has a difficult time understanding him: "...won't have to go to Poland."

"What did you say?"

"That *you* won't have to go to Poland. And that your father and mother and Silvie won't have to go, either."

"How do you know?" She sits down next to him.

"Shhh. It's a big secret. Can you keep a secret until tomorrow? I want to tell you a little of it, because you're so unhappy. But you have to do something for me in return. Will you do that?"

"I don't know."

"Then I won't tell you anything, not even a little bit." Sander stands up, and walks to the door.

"Wait!" Rosa calls. "I'll do what you tell me."

"Come." Sander pulls her onto his lap again.

"What do I have to do?"

"All you have to do is get up. Nothing more. I don't want you staying in bed. All right?"

"Yes."

"Then listen. I've done something for a German general, something that took lots of courage. And because the general was so grateful, he told me I could make a wish. Well, I did. I wished that I didn't have to go to Poland, and that you and Silvie and your parents didn't have to go, either."

"What about Uncle Louis and Aunt Isabelle and Philippe?"

Sander hesitates a moment before answering. "They won't have to go to Poland, either," he says at last. "That's all I'm going to say now. If you keep your promise to me, and get out of bed, I'll tell you the rest of the secret tomorrow. If you don't keep your promise, you won't hear anything more about it. I'll be back at ten o'clock tomorrow morning. We're going downstairs now, and you're not going to say anything about this. Can I trust you?"

"Yes."

"Good. I'm going to the living room, and you are going to wash the tears from your face. Then you are coming downstairs, too."

"You mean we really won't have to go to Poland? Did the general really say that, and—"

"Shhh, not so loud." Sander puts his hand over her mouth.

"No, we won't have to go," he whispers in Rosa's ear. "General Horst von Rabenach told me so himself."

◆ Horst von Rabenach

"Sander will be coming at ten o'clock," says Mama. "Last night he said that he wanted us all to be here, because he had something important to tell us. I have a feeling that he is going into hiding, and that he is coming over to say goodbye."

Rosa is sitting in the big chair. She doesn't say a word. Last night, after she had joined the others in the living room, she did not say much, either, for she was afraid of betraying her uncle's secret. Besides, she wanted to think about Mr. Goldstein some more. She didn't look to see if he was back on the roof again.

"It's almost ten o'clock," says Mama with a sigh. She walks to the window. "There he is," she exclaims. "I'll open the door for him."

Mama returns with her brother a moment later. "Here I am," Sander announces. "Everyone is here, I see. Even Philippe is present. That's good, because what I have to say is very important. No, no coffee for me, Myra, thank you."

Sander coughs. He takes out his handkerchief, and wipes a black smudge off his finger. He coughs again.

"Here we go. Hold on to your seats, everybody, because it's very likely that you won't believe what I'm about to tell you now.

"I want to tell you...that...none of us will have to go to Poland. We have all been exempted from deportation to Poland."

"We're not going to Poland?" Papa grasps the arms of his chair.

"We're not going to Poland. None of us, Herman. You, Myra, and the children won't be going. I won't be going. Louis, Isabelle, and Philippe won't be going, either."

He looks directly at Father. It seems as though Sander is waiting for him to say something. At last Father speaks.

"Is this another one of your fantasies, Sander? Tell me the truth."

"I *am* telling you the truth," Sander replies. "Let me explain what happened.

"One day last week I felt like walking along the Vliet. It was warm, and I was too restless to remain in my studio. When I approached the bridge, I saw a mass of people standing along the side of the water.

"'Someone fell in,' a big man said to me. 'Look, he's drowning. All you can see is his hand.'

"I didn't even think twice. I kicked off my shoes. I was about to remove my jacket, too, when I remembered that if I did so, I wouldn't be wearing a star. Therefore I kept my jacket on. I jumped into the water, and had to dive three times before I was finally able to grab a hand. I pulled, and a head appeared. It was a man, a man in uniform. A German. I was scared to death. I considered letting him drown, but

I couldn't find it in my heart to do that. I held his head above the water, and brought him to the side, where a couple of people took him from me. I snatched my shoes, and ran away in my stockinged feet. I, Sander de Roos, had pulled a German out of the water. That night I was too upset to sleep.

"A Dutch policeman knocked on my door the next morning. 'At precisely eleven o'clock, you must report to General Horst von Rabenach, Paviljoensgracht Twenty-seven, The Hague,' he snarled. I wanted to ask what this was all about, but he had already disappeared.

"I had to hurry. The wind was blowing, and it was raining a little. At five minutes to eleven I was standing at the door of a magnificent old house. I didn't need to ring the bell; the door seemed to open by itself.

"'Go upstairs. The general is expecting you,' said a man in a green uniform. I felt sick to my stomach.

"The man followed me up the steps. He ushered me into a room that was furnished with a large desk. Seated behind the desk was the man I had rescued. He rose, shook my hand, bowed, and clicked his heels together.

"'I am Horst von Rabenach. Please sit down, Mr. de Roos. Do you know why I summoned you?'

"I nodded.

"'We have a good intelligence service. That is why I was able to find out who rescued me yesterday evening. I wish to thank you. I can imagine what was going through your thoughts when you discovered that the person you were fishing out of the water was a German in uniform. You...a Jew.'

"I didn't dare answer. I didn't trust him.

"'Do you know that your fellow Jews from The Hague and the outlying areas are first brought here before being transported to Westerbork?'

"I nodded.

"He bowed. 'I will see to it that you never end up here. I will do this out of gratitude, because you saved my life. How many people do you wish to take with you?'

"'Take with me? Where to?' I was totally confused.

"'To the South of France, to Avignon. I will see to it that you are able to take a number of others with you to Avignon. I have good connections in unoccupied France. You will leave in a couple of days. You will take a train through Belgium, and through the part of France that is already in our hands. Give me the names, addresses, and birth dates of the people you wish to take along! I will write a letter on your behalf, in which I will state that you may go to Avignon as a reward for saving my life.'"

"Just like Ruben's and Rina's grandparents!" Silvie calls. "They fled to Avignon, too, but that's a secret."

"Quiet, Silvie," says Sander, and he waves a large piece of paper. "Who do you think is mentioned in this letter?"

"I am!" Silvie shouts.

Sander begins to dance through the room. "Everyone in this room is mentioned. We're all going to Avignon! Give me your hand, Rosa and Silvie and whoever else wants to join us. We're going to dance on the bridge of Avignon, in freedom!"

"'*Sur le pont d'Avignon ... on y danse ...*'" Aunt Isabelle sings. Mama sings, too.

Sander stops dancing. He stands before Father. "You don't believe me, Herman. It's too good to be true, but it *is* true. This letter came two days after I had been to see Horst von Rabenach. Look!"

They bend over the letter that Sander has in his hands. Printed at the top of the paper is a large bird, an eagle. The paper contains letters that Rosa and Silvie cannot read.

"It's true! It's true!" Mama is laughing and crying at the same time. "The name 'Horst von Rabenach' appears right here, and under his signature, too, but I can't read it very well. Our names and addresses are given. And I see Jossie's and Lita Rosa's names, too. We will all be going to Avignon! How many people are you allowed to take, Sander?"

"Ten, including myself. They must all live in The Hague, or in the surrounding area."

"When are we going, if we go?" asks Father.

"I'll let you know. It won't be long now," Sander answers.

"I will give you French lessons, and we will sing French songs," Aunt Isabelle cheers.

"And I have much to tell you about Avignon," says Uncle Louis. "Isabelle and I have been there many times. It's a splendid city, and very old; the walls surrounding it were built in the Middle Ages. It has a bridge that is so famous that there is a song written about it, '*Sur le pont d'Avignon*,' which Isabelle was just singing. I know it in Dutch. Listen."

He lifts up Philippe, and begins to sing:

> *On the bridge of Avignon,*
> *We'll go dancing, we'll go dancing,*
> *On the bridge of Avignon,*
> *We'll go dancing all around.*

"*Petit Philippe*," he whispers. "We're going to dance on the bridge of Avignon. We'll be free. In Avignon we'll be free."

◆ *Parlez-Vous Français?*

"What animal is pictured on this card?" asks Aunt Isabelle, and she lays a small cardboard square on the table in front of Rosa.

"A cow."

"Good. I'm glad Uncle Louis has drawn it so clearly. Now I want you to find the correct French word."

Rosa examines various cards on which French words are printed. "No, it's not *une pomme*," she says to herself, "and it's not *une table*, either."

"I have it." Rosa sets the card with *une vache* under the picture of the cow.

"Good," says Aunt Isabelle. "Now your turn, Silvie. I want you to find the right card for this one." She lays a picture of a mouse down on the table.

"Here!" Silvie calls. "*Une souris.*"

"You girls are terrific," says Aunt Isabelle. "*Formidable!* When we get to Avignon, it won't be long before you are both speaking fluent French. We'll continue with our lessons there, a couple of hours every day. And you'll go to school again, and to the swimming pool. And—"

"Do we still have our swimming suits and our bathing caps?" Silvie asks.

"Not now, Silvie," Aunt Isabelle answers. "Let's not interrupt the lesson."

The girls put the words under the pictures, making very few mistakes. At the end of the lesson, Aunt Isabelle teaches them a song about moonlight and about Pierrot, who comes to lend a pen:

> *Au clair de la lune*
> *mon ami Pierrot...*

They sing, and they clap their hands. Rosa and Silvie can no longer remain in their seats; they dance through the room. Mama enters with Philippe in her arms.

"None of you heard him crying," she complains. "He has been awake for fifteen minutes."

"Come, Philippe! Dance!" says Rosa, reaching out to him. Philippe almost topples over. She catches him just in time.

"*Sur le pont d'Avignon...Au clair de la lune...*" They sing every French song they know. Uncle Louis has entered the living room, too, and he dances with them. Papa is sitting in the big chair. He doesn't look as serious as usual. Now and then he claps his hands quietly. Philippe chortles.

The doorbell! They stop dancing. Rosa looks from one person to the next. *It seems as though everyone is frozen*, she thinks.

The bell rings again. Father walks to the hall. They hear him opening the door.

Sander's voice. Mama sighs deeply. Aunt Isabelle closes her eyes. They hear footsteps on the stairs.

Sander is standing in the room. "Sit down, everyone, and listen carefully," he says. "I'll come..." He coughs. "I'll come get you tonight. Pack you suitcases. Take some bread with you, and something to drink. I'll be here at seven-thirty, at nineteen hundred thirty hours. If all goes well, we'll be on the train heading for Belgium at a little past eight this evening. I can't stay too long, because in an hour a friend of Horst von Rabenach's will be bringing our travel papers to my studio."

"What kind of clothes should we pack? Is it warm where we're going?"

"Should we wear a star, or not?"

"And my art supplies, what should I do with them?"

"Should we bring money?"

"And food?"

They are all talking at once. Rosa is getting a stomach-ache. She feels nauseated, as well.

"Take as little as possible with you," Sander advises. "Bring only what is absolutely necessary. I'm leaving now. We'll see each other this evening, at nineteen hundred thirty hours. *Adieu.*"

Rosa feels that she is going to be sick. She cups her hands together, and vomits into them.

"Come sit on my lap," Mama whispers. "I don't care if you're dirty."

They walk about in confusion, from upstairs to downstairs, from downstairs to upstairs. Silvie stays in the living room with Philippe, who does nothing but cry. Rosa has cleaned herself up. She is still feeling sick to her stomach. Mama is letting her pack her own suitcase. Later, when she is finished, she will come downstairs and look after Philippe; then Silvie can go upstairs and pack, too.

Underwear, handkerchiefs, skirt, sweater, and a book. Which book? She has so many. It is a shame that she can't pack them all. She chooses *My Name is Theo*, a story about a girl who thinks she is a boy. How strange it is to begin reading a book in Holland, and to finish it in a foreign country! How do you say "My name is Theo" in French?

Her violin. She must not forget her violin. She brings it downstairs, and leaves it in the hall, right by the living room.

They gather around the table. "This is our last dinner in Holland, for the time being," Mama whispers. "Everything must be used up. Aren't you going to eat, Rosa?"

"Leave her alone," says Aunt Isabelle. "I used to get sick to my stomach, too, when I was nervous." She winks at Rosa.

"Avignon is a beautiful city," says Uncle Louis. "It has a splendid papal palace called *Palais des Papes*. And the bridge on which we'll go dancing is called *Pont Saint Bénézet*, and—"

"Stop it, Louis!" Father shouts. His face is so pale that his eyes seem to have turned jet black.

"Don't you have anything else to worry about?" He bows over the table, and brings his face close to Louis's.

"Don't you have anything else to worry about?" Father repeats. "We are all in very great danger. We could still be arrested. And *you* have to play the role of a history teacher. 'Dancing on the bridge of Avignon.' Have you lost your mind? Has this rotten war made you completely insane? Aren't you going to sing that song a few more times for us, that world-famous folk song?" He begins to sing:

"Sur le pont d'Avignon..."

"Don't." Aunt Isabelle begins to cry. "For months we have gotten along so well together. Don't start quarreling now."

Father hangs his head. "I'm sorry," he whispers. "My nerves are getting the best of me."

"We've got to wash the dishes," says Mama. "It's quarter to seven."

"Our suitcases are already downstairs," says Uncle Louis.

"Our suitcases are downstairs, too, and the children's as well," says Papa.

It is fall, yet it is still warm. They are wearing their coats, for it might be cold in the train tonight.

Twenty minutes past seven. They drink one final glass of water. They go to the bathroom one last time. Mama pours bleach into the toilet.

Seven-thirty:
Sander is not here.

Quarter to eight:
Sander is not here.

Eight o'clock:
Sander is not here.

Quarter past eight:
The doorbell.

Father's voice in the hall.
A stranger's voice in the hall.
"Sander has been arrested," says Mama. "I can feel it."

Father returns to the living room. He takes off his coat. "Take your coats off, too!" he calls. "Sander sent his non-Jewish neighbor to us, to say that the travel papers haven't arrived yet. Sander waited until ten minutes to eight, but by that time it was too late for him to go outside. That is all the neighbor said. He disappeared without saying anything more."

Mama leans against a painting of an old narrow street. The street is hanging a bit crooked. "What are we going to do?" she asks.

"Don't you remember that I asked Sander if his story was really true? Don't you remember the suspicions I had?" says Father, and he beats his coat against the sofa. "We've been tricked. Tricked."

"Tomorrow Sander will come to say that everything is all right," says Rosa quietly.

"Our Rosa is a psychic," says Mama, and she laughs a little. "Remember the story of Sander's smoking, and Grandma de Roos's psychic powers? I do believe you have inherited those powers from your grandma."

Rosa doesn't answer. Why is Mama teasing her?

"We may as well go to bed," says Aunt Isabelle. "We'll see what happens tomorrow."

"It's lucky that we made sandwiches to take on the train," says Mama. "At least we'll have something to eat in the morning."

"If the Germans don't come and arrest us tonight," says Papa.

Rosa's stomach is beginning to hurt again.

◆ Departure

Philippe is the only one who slept soundly. For most of the night, Papa sat up with Uncle Louis in the living room. When Rosa heard her father go downstairs, she very quietly crept into bed with her mother. Aunt Isabelle was already lying in Papa's bed, and it wasn't long before Silvie came into the room, too.

During the entire night they lay close to one another, hand in hand. They hardly said a word. Now and then someone sighed, Mama or Aunt Isabelle perhaps. They fell asleep at about four in the morning, and if Philippe had not started to cry, they would be sleeping still.

For breakfast they eat the bread that Mama had packed in her suitcase. They have water with their bread, for there is nothing else in the house to drink.

Aunt Isabelle takes a bottle of milk that she had packed for Philippe, and gives it to him now. "Shall I teach you some more French words after breakfast?" she asks.

"That won't be necessary," says Father loudly. "We're not going to end up in Avignon. Never in my life have I met anyone who could concoct stories the way my brother-in-law Sander can."

"Why don't we go into hiding?" Silvie asks.

"I don't want to, Silvie. I don't want to put other people in danger," Father explains. "If Jews are caught while they're in hiding, the people sheltering them will be sent to a concentration camp, too. And there is treachery all around us. Do you know that the Germans pay money for each Jew who is turned in to them? We are worth seven guilders and fifty cents. Therefore our family is worth thirty guilders." He takes his handkerchief, and wipes the sweat from his forehead.

"That's what Aunt Dien and Uncle Ies said, too," Silvie exclaims. "They didn't want to put other people in danger."

"Who?" says Father, and he wipes his forehead again.

"Never mind."

"We mustn't forget to pick up some more bread at three o'clock this afternoon," says Mama. "We'll put all our coupons together, as we did before. Otherwise we won't have anything to eat when we leave for Avignon tomorrow."

"We're going. We're not going. We're going. We're not going...I'm going to bed for a while," says Father. "I'm exhausted. And all this stress is killing me."

"We *are* going. Here are the papers," says Sander, and he lays a stack of letters on the table. "Here, do you see the date? The train leaves on October seventh, nineteen forty-two, at ten minutes past nine in the morning. What is the date today?"

"It's October sixth," says Mama. "I'll awaken Herman." She runs upstairs.

"Herman, I'll give you your own travel permits, and those of your family," Sander says, when Papa is in the living room. "I'll keep Lita Rosa's and Jossie's papers, and my own, of course. Dear people, I can't stay now. I'll be back tomorrow morning, at about eight-thirty. We should make the most of this day, for it is our last one on Dutch soil, for the time being, at least."

He kisses Mama. "Goodbye, dear sister."

Sander kisses Papa. *He has never done that before*, Rosa thinks.

Sander kisses everyone. He waves, then disappears.

The day drags on. They gather around the table, and talk. The house must be kept neat and orderly now.

"We're getting up at quarter past seven tomorrow morning, and I want the house to be clean and tidy when we leave," says Mama. "I want to show everyone that Jews are clean and orderly people."

They buy their bread at two different bakeries, just as they did two days ago. The de Jongs do not want to arouse any suspicions; they don't want anyone to ask why they need so much bread; they don't want anyone to get the impression that the family might be going away.

They learn a couple of new French words, *une chaise*, a chair. *Un chien*, a dog. They have bread to eat, and water to drink.

At eight o'clock they decide to go to bed. All of them, even the grown-ups. After Rosa has played Philippe to sleep, she brings her violin back to the hall, next to the living room. She must not forget to take her violin. Maybe in France it will be warm enough to play music on the street. A famous violinist might pass by, Yehudi Menuhin, perhaps, and he will be so impressed by her Bartók that he will want to play the violin with her in a concert hall right away. And they will perform on the French radio, too.

Philippe is sleeping. Silvie is sleeping, and the grown-ups are quiet as well.

Rosa is sleeping, too.

The doorbell! Rosa glances at her watch. It is seven o'clock. Sander is already here! Should she go downstairs and open the door for him?

The bell rings again. There is a knock on the door, too, a very loud one that Rosa can hear quite clearly.

She hears Papa walk down the steps. She hears him stop before opening the door in the hall.

"Open that door immediately. Otherwise we'll kick it in!"

There is the sound of many footsteps on the stairs down below. There is the sound of footsteps in the hall by the living room. There are strange voices, and father's voice. Rosa pulls the covers over her head.

"Come on out." Mama is standing next to her bed.

"Wake up, Philippe!" Aunt Isabelle stands by the crib.

"Silvie, get up!" Uncle Louis tries to awaken her.

"Come downstairs, everyone." Papa is in the bedroom, too.

"Have we been arrested?" cries Rosa. "We won't have to go to Poland, will we? Horst von Rabenach will save us."

"Shhh." Father puts his finger to his lips. "A policeman is waiting outside the room," he whispers. "A big fat one. He wouldn't let me come upstairs by myself. They're scared to death that I'll escape. There is another officer downstairs. Come on."

They go down the steps. Aunt Isabelle has Philippe in

her arms. Walking behind Isabelle is a policeman, a fat, greasy-looking Dutchman.

They enter the living room. "Sit down," says the officer who has remained downstairs. "You take the big chair, my good colleague."

"That's Papa's chair," says Silvie.

"She's an insolent little brat, isn't she?" The fat policeman rests his hands on the arms of Papa's chair. A cigar is dangling between his fingers. He puts the cigar in his mouth, and begins to speak.

"I'll give you forty-five minutes to get dressed. Adults first, then the children. And remember, no tricks. No throwing any personal possessions to the neighbors downstairs. Everything in this house belongs to the German authorities now. *Heil Hitler!*" He stands, and raises his right arm. "*Heil Hitler,* colleague! Where are you?"

"*Heil Hitler!*" shouts the other policeman. "The adults and the baby are to go upstairs first, then the children. Hurry!"

Rosa and Silvie are alone in the room with the two officers. A policeman's cap is resting on Philippe's high-chair.

Rosa is shaking so badly that she must grab her one hand with the other in order to stop. She doesn't want the men to see how terrified she is.

The fat man looks at her. He begins to laugh. "Take a look at this, Kram," he says. "The children are even more nervous than their parents."

"Idiot!" answers the other. "You called me by name. Fool!"

"It doesn't matter if these brats know that our names are Kram and Balland. In another couple of weeks, they won't be able to repeat a thing." He draws his finger across his throat in a cutting motion. "They'll all be dead...*kaput!*"

"Mama!" Silvie screams. Rosa screams, too.

"Upstairs!" shouts the fat man. "And hurry up. You have twenty minutes."

"We have twenty minutes," Rosa sobs, when she is upstairs. "And we'll all be dead, he said. But that's not true, because we have letters from the general. If we didn't have those papers, I would open the balcony doors and jump to the neighbors below. I would jump down to Mrs. Bazuin."

"Don't even think of it. I must deliver you safe and sound to the police station on the Herenstraat," says the fat officer. "Now get ready. You have fifteen more minutes." He sits down on Rosa's bed.

"He followed us upstairs," Silvie wails.

"Get dressed," the man snarls. "You have ten more minutes."

"Put on your warm clothes," says Mama. "Three pairs of underpants, and the warmest dress you have. Rosa, you wear that yellow one from Het Kleine Paradijs, and Silvie, you wear—"

"I'll put my pillow in my pants," cries Silvie. "Then I won't feel anything if they beat me."

"Five more minutes!" shouts the officer.

"Rotten traitor," Papa whispers.

"Did you say something, you dirty little Jew?"

"No."

"Three more minutes.

"Two more minutes.

"One more minute...

"Downstairs, everyone. Forward...march!"

◆ From A to Z

They cross the Broekslootkade in a small procession. Aunt Isabelle walks in front, followed by Uncle Louis, who has Philippe in his arms. Papa and Mama come next, then Rosa and Silvie. The fat policeman leads the group; the other officer walks behind them. They must move along at a brisk pace, like soldiers. Now and then Rosa leans her violin case against her shoulder. It feels much heavier than usual.

"Don't forget to take your violin," Mama said. "Maybe you can play for Philippe when we're at the police station. We will most likely receive special treatment because of Horst von Rabenach. When the officials at the station see our papers, they will certainly let us go right home."

"One, two, three...halt!" The officer in front raises his hand. "Stop and wait for the other group!"

They are standing in front of the hairdresser's. A girl working in the shop window is holding the head of a mannequin in her hand. Rosa hardly dares to look at that bald head. Fortunately, the girl covers it with a black wig.

Another policeman is marching in the distance. By squinting a little, Rosa can see that there are people walking behind him. Children, too. She can hear their footsteps as they approach. Hanna and Ruth van Gich are among that group. Someone on crutches is walking behind Hanna. *That's right*, Rosa thinks. *That is Grandpa van Gich. He had a stroke a couple of months ago, and he can't walk very well now. How pitiful he looks.*

"Forward...march!" The policeman in front begins to move on. The two groups merge. Four policemen are escorting them now.

They come to the Herenstraat. They march past the Magneet, the Sierkan, the library, and Van Woerden.

They pass a man who is walking his dog. They watch a woman as she pours water on the sidewalk.

"See you this evening," they hear a man call. He mounts his bicycle, and waves to a woman with a big stomach.

"She has a baby in there," Silvie whispers.

"Shut up!" a policeman shouts to her.

A butcher steps outside his shop across the street. He stands with his hands on his hips as he watches the procession pass. The sight of his blood-stained apron is making Rosa feel sick to her stomach. She looks away.

"Keep going!" An officer grabs Grandpa van Gich by the arm. "If you were on your way to the market to earn money from your antique stall there, you would be walking faster, old man!"

The other policemen laugh.

They arrive at the police station. The officers push them inside.

The church clock rings the hour. Rosa doesn't know how many times the chimes have sounded; she is too nauseated to count.

They proceed upstairs. "This is where you are to go, you Jews." A man in a green uniform points to an open door.

They enter a large room. Colored portraits are hanging on the walls. A blond German officer wearing black boots and a green uniform is sitting on a table.

"Remain standing!" he calls. "Move forward! Many more of your kind will be coming. Our goal is sixty today. Close in. This hall is going to be filled with Jewish men and women, and we don't have that much space!" He rubs his hands together.

The de Jongs are standing near the table, right by the German. Rosa can smell the polish on his boots. The gleaming insignia on his cap, a death's head, has been polished as well.

People are continually streaming in. Their voices buzz together in confusion. Philippe begins to cry. Another baby cries, too.

"Rosa! Silvie!" Lita Rosa's voice.

Rosa turns around. Lita Rosa and Jossie are standing at the other end of the room, next to the door.

"Hello! Keep your chin up. Remember our general. Long live Horst von Rabenach!" Lita Rosa waves her papers in the air.

"*Maul halten!*" shouts the German.

When he shouts, he looks like the men in the pictures that are hanging on the wall, Rosa thinks.

The room becomes quiet. The Dutch policemen scattered throughout the crowd are standing with their legs wide apart, and their hands behind their backs.

"The head of each family must report to me," calls the German officer. "I'll start with the letter A."

"What did he say?" The voice of Grandpa van Gich is coming from somewhere in the middle of the hall.

"Don't you understand Dutch? Yes, you there, with those crutches. Don't I speak Dutch well?"

"Yes. Oh yes, sir."

"Louder! 'You speak Dutch very well, Herr Lieutenant.' That is what I want to hear!"

"You...you speak Dutch very well, Herr Lieutenant," Grandpa van Gich calls.

"Children there!" The lieutenant points to the left. "*Erwachsene* there!" His hand moves to the right. "When the head of the family reports, he must indicate to me who his children are. Understand? Take your places now!"

Everyone starts to move at the same time. The children form a line. "The biggest ones here, the smallest ones there," says an officer, and he begins to pull the children toward their proper places. "Remain standing!" he snaps to a girl in a blue-and-red-checked dress.

"*Ruhe!* I want it quiet now!" The German crosses his legs. "Van den Akker. Step up. Report!"

A little man comes forward. He looks like Mr. Goldstein.

"Hat off!" shouts the lieutenant. "You people don't even know the meaning of the word *courtesy*. Take that hat off!"

The little man stands with his hat in his hands.

"Who are your children?"

"That is Baruch, and that is Channele." He points.

"I don't care what you call them. Keep your ghetto names to yourself. Save them for Poland. There are lots of ghetto names in Poland. Is your wife here?" The German points to the people in the room.

The little man nods.

"Four!" shouts the lieutenant to one of the policemen. "Write it down!"

He calls the next name. "Barends!"

A large man approaches the table.

"Who are your children, or don't you have any?"

"No."

"Plus one. No children! Write it down!"

He calls the next name. "Cohen. I'm expecting a stampede now. You Jews are all named Cohen, aren't you?" The German slaps his knee with laughter. All the policemen laugh with him.

A woman reports to the table.

"Go back to your place. I asked for the head of the family to come forward."

"*I* have been the head of the family these past two months." The woman stands up very straight. "And those are my children." She points to a big boy and a little girl.

"Do you know what happened to the head of the family?" she continues. "He died of pneumonia in Mauthausen. Don't make me laugh. Pneumonia. He was murdered. By you Germans!" She points to the lieutenant. "You Nazis murdered him, the father of my children!"

"Bring her to the waiting room for now!" shouts the German. "Insolent Jew. You go with her!" He points to her children. "To the waiting room with you!"

With bowed heads the boy and girl follow their mother.

"Cohen! Moos Cohen! Saar Cohen, Bram Cohen."

No one reports to the table.

"Denneboom!"

An old man steps forward.

"Elzas, Emmerick, Edelstein! Finkenberg, Fröhlich…"

The lieutenant finally comes to the letter *J*.

"De Jong."

Papa and Jossie report to the table. "Those two girls are my children. In that yellow woolen dress, and in that red sweater," says Papa, wiping his forehead.

"Are you hot?" asks the German officer, and he begins to laugh. "I can tell you that something most unusual is happening today. By noontime the temperature will be above seventy-two degrees, beach weather."

He puts on his cap. The death's head insignia is directly above his nose. "I have one comforting thought for you: It won't be as hot in Poland. The following with the letter *J*."

"Papa, remember Horst von Rabenach!" Rosa would like to call.

Before she can say a word, her father takes the papers out of his pocket. He hands them to the German.

"What is this?"

"These are our travel permits for the South of France, for Avignon."

The lieutenant stands, and holds the papers up to the light.

"We received these permits from General Horst von Rabenach," Jossie explains. "The general was rescued by Sander de Roos, his brother-in-law." Jossie points to Father. "Sander pulled Horst von Rabenach out of the water, and as a reward—"

"Worthless. They're worthless papers," sneers the German.

There is the sound of paper tearing, of men laughing. The lieutenant throws the shreds up into the air. They whirl down to the floor like snowflakes.

"No!" Rosa screams. "Don't!"

Father does not move. Jossie rejoins the others.

"Back to your place!" A policeman grabs Father by the shoulder. Father walks as if in a daze.

Silvie tiptoes to her sister. She slips her hand into Rosa's hand.

"Go back, little de Jong. You must stand in line according to height." An officer returns Silvie to her place. "You must stand in the correct order," he says.

Rosa feels as if she is going to be sick. She has a bitter taste in her mouth. She swallows.

"Don't throw up," says Lientje, who is standing next to her. "Take some deep breaths."

"How many so far?" the German asks the officer who is writing down the census.

"Forty," the officer replies. "Twenty more to go. We'll make it. We haven't processed *K* through *Z* yet."

Rosa looks at Lientje, who is holding something in her hand. It takes a while before Rosa can see that Lientje is grasping a bunch of colored threads. Hanging from each thread is a tiny doll, an elf with a brightly colored hat on its head.

"My mother saved these for me," Lientje whispers. "They came in boxes of soap powder. I'm giving an elf to each child here. It's something to remember me by."

Lientje puts her hand behind her back. "Take one and pass them down," she whispers.

Rosa looks at the German, who is talking to a man in a blue coat.

"Pass them down," she hears the children at the end of the line whisper.

The German lights a cigarette with a gold lighter. He inhales deeply. Smoke comes out of his nose.

"*Einliefern!*" he shouts. "Turn in all the *Heinzelmännchen*. I saw you passing them down. Give them to me!"

He walks down the line. Each child puts an elf in his hand.

"Filthy swine!" Rosa hears Lita Rosa's voice. Lita Rosa pushes her way through the crowd until she is standing in front of the German officer.

"Filthy swine!" she calls again. "You Nazis take everything away from us, even those harmless little elves...free in boxes of soap powder."

The German throws his cigarette butt on the floor. He steps on the sparks. "There is no place for toys in Westerbork and in Poland," he says. "Take your place. *Schnell!*"

Lita Rosa remains standing. She does not look like Lita Rosa anymore. Her lips are pressed tightly together, and her eyes are half closed.

"Bastard!" She spits at the German. Rosa shuts her eyes.

She hears the sounds of a beating. There is a final blow. A thud. Then silence. Rosa opens her eyes.

Lita Rosa is sprawled out on the floor. She is lying next to a huge dead butterfly, her purple hair bow. Blood is pouring from her nose.

"Bring that insolent Jew to the waiting room," says the lieutenant, as he lights another cigarette.

Two policemen come forward. They grab Lita Rosa under her arms, and pull her to her feet.

"Walk," a policeman commands. "Forward, march!"
Lita Rosa's legs are dragging along the floor.
"Forward, march!"

◆ Waltz of the Clouds

They must all proceed to the waiting room now. Every
letter of the alphabet has been called.

"Sixty-four!" the policeman announced, and the German
told him that he was more than satisfied with the number.

There goes Papa. Mama follows with Silvie. Rosa walks
behind her sister. All the policemen have left the room.

"Come here, you!"

Rosa would like to keep walking.

"Come here, you!"

Someone is holding her back. She looks behind her. It
is the German officer.

"Stay here." He closes the door.

"Do you know why you are the only one I've kept back?"

"No."

"Because you look just like my little daughter. Here she
is." He removes a leather case from the breast pocket of
his uniform. He takes out a photograph, and touches it to
his lips.

"Look, that is Wendela, my little daughter, my treasure,
the light of my life. Do you see that she looks like you? Sweet,
isn't she, posing with her violin."

"I want to go to my father and mother. I want to go with them to Westerbork and to Poland."

"The trucks are making other stops before coming here. They won't arrive for some time yet. How did your father get those permits from Horst von Rabenach, anyway? I've never heard of that general. Those papers are worthless."

Rosa does not answer.

"I see that you have your violin with you. You must play for me. Take out your violin, and play what you want. Don't wait. You must play for me right now. I'm crazy about violin music, especially romantic music."

Rosa opens her violin case. How strange. She can hear Mr. Goldstein's voice. She looks at the ceiling, but Mr. Goldstein is not there. She looks at the walls of the room, but all she can see are the colored portraits of strong blond men.

"Play Gideon's waltz," Mr. Goldstein whispers.

"Can you play a waltz?" asks the German. "How long have you been taking lessons?"

"Over three years."

"Just like Wendela. She is ten. Are you ten years old, too?"

"Yes."

"Whenever I hear a waltz, I am reminded of long white ball gowns, and red wine in crystal glasses."

Rosa begins to play. Her hands are shaking.

"Good," says Mr. Goldstein. "But don't be so nervous, Rosa. Look at him. Open your eyes."

The German is sitting on the table. His eyes are closed. He sways to the beat of the music.

The waltz is over. "Repeat," Mr. Goldstein whispers. "*Da capo al fine!*"

The sound of the waltz reverberates through the room once again.

"Bravo!" The German claps his hands. "You play just as beautifully as Wendela. That piece was by Mozart, wasn't it?"

"No, it was by Goldstein. 'Waltz of the Clouds' by Gideon Goldstein."

The German jumps off the table. He grasps her by the shoulders. "Get out of here!" he hisses. "Disappear! You can leave by the fire escape. We have enough Jews for today."

"I want to be with my Mama!"

"When you play the violin, you look like Wendela," he says. "And when you cry, you look like her, too." He pats her on the head.

"Get going, I tell you." He opens a door. "You'll end up at the side of the station. Walk straight ahead, then turn left. You'll be on the Herenstraat again. Get out before the trucks arrive!" He pushes her toward the fire escape.

"Mama!" she calls.

"Don't cry," Mr. Goldstein whispers. "Go, or I'll push you down the stairs myself!"

She runs down the fire escape. Mr. Goldstein must have pushed her hard. Walk straight ahead...turn left.

"Rosa! How did *you* get here?"

There is Sander. He is walking with a suitcase in his hand.

"I was on my way to join you," he says. "I saw you and your family coming down the street and entering the station. I thought to myself, *if everyone has been captured, what am*

I going to do by myself in the South of France? I'll go report to the police station, too. And now I see you out on the street, all of a sudden. Did you escape?"

She nods.

Sander takes her by the hand. "Rosa, let's get away before the trucks arrive. Run as fast as you can. Run, Rosa! *Run!*"

◆ *Epilogue*

Rosa, Sander, Jossie, Uncle Izak, and Mr. Rozeboom survived the war. All the rest of the Jews you met in this book, adults and children, perished before the liberation.

After the war, Sander and Rosa neither wished to, nor were they able to, talk about what happened to them after Rosa had fled from the police station.

Rosa came to live with Sander after the liberation in 1945. They were a comfort to each other, and together they could mourn the loss of all their loved ones.

Sander is married to Ineke, who was his classmate at the art academy. They moved to the United States, where Sander found work as an advertising designer. Sander and Ineke have a daughter, whom they named Silvie.

Upon graduation from the Music Conservatory in Rotterdam, Rosa left Holland as well. She is a violinist in the Israel Philharmonic Orchestra.

When she has a free evening, she will occasionally perform with her husband, Jona Barnheim, and their children, Dina and Isha. The billboard announcing their program might look like this:

The Barnheim Quartet

will play the string quartets
No. 1 and No. 4 by

Béla Bartók

Jona Barnheim—cello
Dina Barnheim—viola
Isha Barnheim—violin
Rosa Rosevici—violin

◆ Author's Note

My own wartime experiences provided the background for much of this book. I used real people as models for many of my characters. The de Jongs, for example, were patterned after my family. Maurits, Mally, and little Johnny van Voolen, who moved in with us just before they were deported to the camps, became Louis, Isabelle, and petit Philippe Mendes. The idea behind the story, however, was not inspired by actual fact, but by a rumor that spread through our community and offered us a glimmer of hope during the dark days of the occupation. The central figure in this rumor was a man named Friedrich Weinreb.

Weinreb was born into an orthodox Jewish family in Poland in 1910. Pogroms forced the family to flee to Holland in 1916. They settled in Scheveningen, a city that was already home to many Eastern European Jews. Young Weinreb enrolled at the Netherlands School of Economics in Rotterdam, and earned a master's degree in 1938. He enjoyed great distinction because of his orthodox way of life, his intelligence, and his ability to handle difficult situations. He was regarded as a sort of *wonderrebbe*, a learned and respected teacher. It was only natural that the Jewish community would rely on his wisdom and judgment after the Germans overran Holland in 1940.

The deportation of Jews began early in 1942. Men and women over the age of sixteen were ordered to report to work camps. Unaware that they were being sent to their deaths, a great number of Jews complied. Some people ignored the order and went into hiding. Others tried to stall for time and asked Weinreb to help them seek deferments.

As conditions under the Nazi regime grew more oppressive, rumors about the powers of this *wonderrebbe* began to spread. In perhaps the most fantastic rumor of all, it was reported that Weinreb had saved the life of the German lieutenant general von Schumann by pulling him from the path of an oncoming automobile. As a reward, Weinreb was to be given the opportunity to take a number of Jews to the South of France. Weinreb himself compiled a list of all the people he planned to lead to safety.

My family and I were among those on "the Weinreb list." I wasn't allowed to tell anyone about it. We learned French words, sang French songs, and waited each day for news of our departure, which never came. My mother had become suspicious of this list, and finally convinced my father that going into hiding was our only hope for survival. After the war, we learned that almost everyone on the list who had not gone into hiding had died in the camps.

To this day, no one knows the real story behind the Weinreb list. The only certainty is this: Friedrich Weinreb led a group of desperate people to believe that the day would come when they would reach the South of France and leave deportation and death far behind them.